THEY TURNED ... REVENGE INTO A NIGHTMARE OF ESCALATING HORROR.

Lisa—Beneath her startling beauty lived a cunning tigress, aroused by danger, capable of a desperate act that would stun the world.

Phillip—His good looks and easy charm masked deep scars and a sadistic need to avenge a secret wrong.

John—A rugged, hard-hitting undercover agent, he had nearly fit the pieces together when a sensual woman with a dangerous past scrambled the board.

Dr. Lewis—A nuclear expert, he was the first to realize the appalling danger. But when he went to the FBI, no one would listen. Millions of lives would depend on . . .

THE CALIFORNIA FACTOR

THE CALIFORNIA FACTOR

Patricia Vernier

A DELL BOOK

Published by
Dell Publishing Co., Inc.
1 Dag Hammarskjold Plaza
New York, New York 10017

Dell ® TM 681510, Dell Publishing Co., Inc.

ISBN: 0-440-10989-2

Printed in Canada
First printing—November 1980

Dedicated to the one I love.

The author wishes to express her warmest gratitude to Joyce, Kay, and Frank, and to her editors, Sandi Gelles-Cole and Kathy Sagan.

PROLOGUE

In the gray winter dusk sheets of rain sprayed the sidewalks of Union Square, and Mary Rose Stoval dodged the muddy puddles, her lungs sucking in the frigid air which bit at the back of her palate. With the palm of her sodden glove she wiped her forehead, the sides of her nose, and the top of her lip. Her flimsy plastic poncho snapped in the wind, and she chided herself for not getting something better than this button-up cleaner's bag.

In a way that had become routine for her, she checked over her shoulder to make sure that no one was following. Fear and anxiety wore at her strength, aggravating her hunger. She tried to remember when she had last eaten and thought back to the day before yesterday at the same time fingering her only coins to see if they had changed into something that would buy a meal.

Hunched beneath the protection of their umbrellas, the shoppers were loaded down with parcels. Their absorption in the bright window decorations denied the reality of anything outside the holiday routine.

Lulled, Mary Rose slowed to a walk and allowed

herself to be carried along past I. Magnin down Stockton to Macy's. A display of toys and elves in the window caught her eye, reminding her that today, the twenty-fourth, was also Christmas Eve. Somehow she was always surprised when Christmas finally arrived after the months of heralding. A lump in her throat threatened to choke off her breath. She kept swallowing nervously as a defense against caring too much. . . .

With a final check over her shoulder she pushed through the double doors and worked her way along the crowded aisles, up an escalator to a second-floor restroom where she locked herself in one of the stalls. Sagging against the wall, she permitted herself a moment's rest, then dug into her purse for the roll of blue jeans and sneakers she had brought to change into from her slacks and five-inch platform heels. With a pocket mirror propped on the fold-down shelf she removed the blond wig, brown contact lenses, and porcelain-toned makeup.

As she was peeling off the false eyelashes, she was startled to see a little boy's face appear sideways under the door. His tiny eyes stared with curiosity until he was swooped up and admonished by a mothering voice never to look under a bathroom door again. In a fit of frantic giggles Mary Rose cupped her hand over her mouth and warned herself not to attract attention, torturing herself into sobriety with visions of being caught. Fear wrenched her empty stomach as the bars of a prison cell appeared against the mat of her eyelids as if in a photographic negative, making her dizzy despite the proof of her safety. Forcing the bolt lock, she burst from the cubicle and startled a woman at the towel dispenser, who froze with dripping hands. Transfixed by Mary Rose's panic, the woman offered a nod of sympathy, then fished her purse off the floor and scurried away.

Mary Rose held on to the sink until the waves of nausea passed. Maybe she should have kept her disguise; she always felt safer behind the mask of a false identity, as bold as a kid on Halloween. Was her plan doomed? She stared at herself in the mirror, startled by the apprehensive eyes, the pale, fat face, the frizzy black mane. She tried a smile, but out came a grimace. Ducking her head close to the bowl, she splashed her cheeks until she felt calm enough to face the Christmas crowds.

No one gave her a second glance as she walked to the elevator and rode down to the ground floor along with a little girl who was promising her father that she would mow the lawn until New Year's if she could keep the present they had just bought for her brother. Over his child's head the man flashed Mary Rose an amused smile, and she forced herself to return it. She knew this would be the most difficult part—blending in with the crowd, accepting the innocence of her appearance, and remaining calm when someone looked at her.

Once outside she walked over to Market and headed south on Third. Rain soaked through the toes of her sneakers and oozed insidiously along her bare feet. She considered going into a bakery to warm up, tempted by the aroma of frying doughnuts, but the place was deserted, and she was leary of drawing the counterman's attention. Instead she kept walking with her head down against the wind, bullying herself into staying alert with reminders that anything might happen. Things had a way of suddenly turning violent, particularly in the city with all the people rushing around. She couldn't tell what a person might take it into his head to do.

From across the street she was hailed by a pair of teen-aged boys in quilted windbreakers, their words obscured, but their tone clearly obscene. A flicker of excitement stirred her defenses. The idea of a confrontation seemed to promise a release. Reaching into her purse, she touched the .22-caliber semi-automatic and thought about pulling it on a couple of creeps like them just to see the looks on their faces. Suddenly she felt invincible.

On first examination the pistol had seemed too light, and the one-ounce slug, a pellet for target shooting. But now its leanness appealed to her; it could be almost completely silenced.

With a tinge of regret she looked back over her shoulder and saw that the boys were continuing on, as if sensing she would be an impossible prey. She imagined herself projecting an aura of deadly power and cunning sexuality which insured that only the steeliest of men would dare to approach.

At Harrison she stopped at the Pacific telephone building and descended to the empty courtyard located below street level and decorated by three life-size sculptures. The bronze miners seemed absorbed in their work, reassuring in their silent steadiness. But she remained troubled by a nagging worry that maybe she shouldn't have come at all. Fear seeped into her pores. She tried bolstering her composure by reviewing her plans, but her strategies seemed empty now; she would have to act on the impulse of the moment.

Looking back to the level of the street, she considered leaving, but the ache in her belly convinced her to stay and accept the risk.

The building was closed for the night, the lobby dark and empty. But as extra protection she edged into the shrubbery which surrounded the sculptures and waited beside the figure of an old man who was stooped by the trickling stream with a gold pan in hand. Her pulse picked up; she breathed deeply through parted lips. Why was she suddenly so frightened? Her feelings were running a giddy gamut from terror to invincibility and back. Her pulse throbbed. She wondered if she were making a mistake in trusting the doctor. She'd never been right to trust anyone before, but she was so tired of being alone and scared. Her fear gave her a look of weakness which people seemed to pick up on.

Hearing the tap of high heels, she looked up at the sidewalk and saw the doctor gliding past looking slim and beautiful in a sleek raincoat, her auburn hair flying beneath a white umbrella that framed her head like a halo.

As the doctor paused and looked down into the courtyard, Mary Rose was suddenly conscious of her own piggish bulk and mangy black hair. She was tempted to remain in hiding, but the doctor was coming down the steps with an impatience that seemed to demand satisfaction, so Mary Rose stepped away from the shrubs. She felt as if bees were trapped beneath her skin, buzzing back and forth, turning her organs to soft wax. She decided to stick to her plan—it would be okay. There wasn't time to think of anything else. Whatever happened, happened—for better or worse. She could only plan so far. But when she met the doctor's eyes, something contracted and burst inside her. Ripples of chills spilled from her chin to her knees. The tension was too high, the conflict too strong. Right away she felt it all going wrong. She had badly miscalculated; they were strangers. All the rapport was gone; it wasn't working out here in the open with the pressure of the wind and rain and hollow darkness.

Operating by rote, Mary Rose explained her problems to the doctor—her obsessive fear of capture, her terrible need for money and a place to stay—almost gleefully trying to shock a response from that cool facade, like a kid peeling away a Band-Aid to reveal a gruesome scab.

But the doctor's eyes closed with annoyance, as if confronted with a movie already seen and disliked. Always the conscientious professional, she tried to justify her unwillingness to help, but Mary Rose couldn't seem to listen. She was fixated on the refusal, the reasons didn't matter. Why did this madwoman think that reasons mattered?

She grew dizzy from the hostile logic—the words of an enemy. And then suddenly the bitch was finished; she was going and leaving Mary Rose alone in the night. . . . As casually as one might call out an apology, Mary Rose reached into her purse and squeezed the trigger of the pistol to shoot directly through the leather.

The doctor fell twisted to one side, her face exposed to the rain in a puddle that grew rosy with blood. Her crumpled body looked so lost on the concrete expanse that Mary Rose grabbed it under the arms and dragged it into the seclusion of the shrubbery to lie at rest under the guardianship of the old man by the stream, with her head cradled in the gold pan as if on a pillow.

Staring at the contorted face, she felt a cavity open within her, admitting the frigid air to whistle around in her hollow limbs, to freeze her brain from the inside out. She felt remote and objective, as if previously recorded instructions were insuring her preservation.

To create the illusion of a mugging, she removed the doctor's watch, purse, and diamond ring. Her intention was to drop them in the trash somewhere, but once in hand they held a strange fascination. The wallet's identification seemed an answered prayer, an offering of the doctor's discarded cloak of identity.

Tugging at the limp body, she worked off the trench coat and exchanged it for her plastic poncho, which she tucked around the doctor like a protective blanket. The coat's cloth was rough to the touch, the tailoring second-rate, and she wondered why the doctor couldn't afford something better. Nevertheless she was pleased by her reflection in the building window. Of course the belt refused to close over her fat stomach, but still it felt fine.

She wiggled the ring onto her little finger, snapped

on the watch, and slung the purse over her shoulder. Flipping back her hair, she picked up the fallen white umbrella and was warmed by its brightness. With a sense of wonder she felt her fear subside.

ONE

The mountain road cut up from the Pacific Coast highway in Malibu at a steep incline, suggesting that the engineers had preferred a simple, straight line over the top. The banks of the cliffs were rooted with ice plant to anchor the soil against the driving California rains, and down in the ravine off the other side could be seen the rusted hulk of an automobile that had missed a turn.

Cautiously Phillip took his eyes off the road and saw that Lisa gripped the steering wheel as if it were a ledge over a precipice.

"Nervous?"

At the sound of his voice she bolted in her seat, wove the van over the center line, and jerked it precariously back into her lane. The hard set to her mouth disowned her jumpiness.

"Just get what you can and get out," he said. "No risks. If it looks bad, you just leave, okay?"

She frowned at the empty reassurance, and he felt conniving for having tried. Of course there would be risk. She was chewing on her plump lower lip, and despite the dowdy disguise her fear gave her a strange beauty. Her skin was translucent and pale with flushes of color at the cheekbones. Her slanting, almost Oriental eyes squinted out the breeze, and her nostrils flared as if to pick out the scent of a direction.

A few miles further on the road finally leveled off, with offshoots to eclectic, owner-built homes and scattered ranches and farms. Hunched down in the passenger seat, Phillip tried to allay his panic with reminders that in all likelihood he would be back in his office by the afternoon, safely absorbed in paperwork at his desk. But his succor failed; his stomach ached like a raw wound. Would he always be plagued by last-minute doubts that reduced his schemes to niggling fears?

Slowing at the intersection, Lisa turned into the road leading to the plateau of the Rancho Verde shopping center, a group of shops catering to the affluent Malibu locals and tourists at the adjoining Malibu Sands Hotel. She pulled behind the sprawling building, stopped at the rear of a Baskin-Robbins ice-cream store, and turned to Phillip with a kind of sick finality.

"So I guess this is it, hotshot."

He wet his lips and tasted the awful chemical tang of the skin bronzer coating his face and neck, then shoved aside strands of the black wig that were plastered to his forehead with perspiration. Out his window he caught a slash of ocean far in the distance glinting like a livid layer of smog at the horizon.

"You all right?" he asked.

A stiff nod. She looked almost faint with tension. As if to distract herself, she smoothed her full-length, gathered skirt. Specially constructed, it was triple-sewn, with a reinforced nylon waistband and a heavy steel clasp. Hidden in the folds of the cloth were pockets marked at the corners by plastic beads in the manner of a magician's scarf.

To lighten her mood he nodded at the voluminous cloth. "It makes you look like a hippo."

"Oh dear." She fluttered her eyelids. "And I was so hoping to get laid on this job."

He smiled. "Just take it easy."

"Sure."

"But, Lisa . . ."

"Yeah?"

"Try for a critical mass?" After winning her smile he pulled on his sunglasses and climbed out.

As the van drove away, he was alarmed to spot a slight fuzz at the bottom of one of the hand-painted logos on the rear door where a hair of the brush had strayed. But he knew that no one would notice; the van was indistinguishable from the one he had used for a guide.

He strolled to the hotel and slowed for a tour through the plush lobby. His baggy sweat shirt drew a few glances, but he ignored the fashionable guests and took the elevator up to the top floor and then a staircase up to the roof. In a blaze of sunlight he opened the door and saw with immediate relief that the roof was deserted, as usual. The raised sun deck was covered with peeling linoleum, surrounded by a dozen chaise longues. In the stale breeze the torn plastic webbing fluttered above a scattering of Schlitz cans.

At the edge of the building he checked out the kids splashing in the pool fifteen stories below while their parents lay comatose on umbrella-shaded lounges. Tiers of balconies went down the side of the hotel like a ladder—tiny outcroppings of concrete which appeared to have been designed more for the benefit of window washers than guests. He imagined himself making the straight drop, and with a roughness that precluded further thought he yanked off his sweat shirt and strode to the opposite side of the roof.

One hundred feet of nylon rope encircled his chest in twin bandoliers, which he uncoiled into a lank heap. From where he stood, he could look down on the Consolidated Atomic complex and the sprawling grounds which abutted the hotel property at an ivy-covered, chain link fence topped with three strands of innocuous barbed wire. The concrete and steel buildings, painted a benign peach, gave the appearance of a university campus. In the garage area down by the experimental reactor the men unloading at the dock kept to a slow and easy pace—like workers everywhere, in no hurry to finish the job. They seemed unaware that beyond the opened double doors on a pair of movable carts sat a dozen coffee-can-size containers of uranium oxide with nearly two-thirds the amount of uranium 235 in the Hiroshima bomb, valued in excess of one million dollars.

The neglected wooden sign in front of the brick wall was shrouded by an overgrowth of ivy, but a hexagonal logo enclosing the block letters CA and some faded red capitals warning, *Danger, Contami-*

nated Water, were visible between the leaves. Towering eucalyptus lined the road, and bright beds of marigolds contributed to the atmosphere of casual creativeness, a calculated effort on the part of the architects to play down the dangers of nuclear power while portraying atomic fission as a controlled and domesticated process—a beast whose spirit had been broken once and for all.

Beyond the guard booth the only apparent security of the inner compound was another chain link fence, making it seem a friendly, everyday place—as congenial as a modern shopping center. Men in jeans pedaled bicycles along the roads within the fence, and the people strolling the paths talked and laughed with an animation that ruled out professional concerns.

Hoping that their easygoingness disposed them to accept strangers, Lisa pulled behind a string of vehicles lined up at the entrance's stop signs and flashing lights. She noticed a preference for what she called "university cars," staid Audies, Volkswagens, and Toyotas, each of them bearing a CA sticker on the bumper, their drivers identified by little plastic photo badges.

In an impulsive final chock she unfolded a xeroxed floor plan, knowing full well that further study wouldn't help her. Already she could draw the area in her sleep; the rest was beyond her control. Those neatly labeled rectangles, which looked so clear-cut and safe on paper, were rooms teeming with life and fraught with danger—rooms where anything at all might happen.

When the traffic advanced, she followed along. The

day was too warm for gloves, so she shielded her fingerprints with rubber cement and had to keep stretching her fingers to keep them apart.

On approaching the guard she worried that the camouflage of her oversized sunglasses might provoke suspicion. The long bangs of a brown wig hung down past her eyebrows to hide most of her face, and a tight bra beneath a baggy blouse completely eclipsed her breasts to prevent even casual glances of sexual interest. But in spite of her worry about overdoing it, she was comforted by the disguise. It seemed a wall to keep her safe, boosting her courage for risks that otherwise might overwhelm her.

The guard sat on a little stool just inside the booth, looking bored by the routine of waving through the regulars; but as Lisa approached, he rose and flashed her a reminder to stop. A diminutive man in his early sixties with a graying toothbrush mustache, he appeared to see his function as little more than directing traffic.

She rolled down the window and tried to match his boredom. "Telegram."

He brightened with curiosity. "What's with the truck?"

"It's a company van." Nervously she glanced at the roof of the Malibu Sands Hotel. Was it possible that Phillip's meticulous Western Union logos looked fake?

The man scratched his moustache. "I thought the trucks caught so much flak for bad-news telegrams that the company had you drive your own cars."

Clenched around the wheel, her cemented fingers stuck tight. She snapped away her thumb. "I blew a head gasket, so they made me a loan."

"Well, this one looks reliable enough."

As he scrutinized the van, she moved restlessly on the seat, her mind beginning to cloud with fear. She hadn't planned on encountering a talker; Phillip would be waiting.

Sensing her impatience, he inclined his head toward the telegram on the dashboard. "Want to leave it here?"

"It's collect—for the dispatcher."

"Oh, you want the loading dock then." He pointed out an interior road and started a chatty series of directions.

"I know where it is," she cut in, easing her foot from the brake. Phillip would be anxious; she was already six minutes overdue.

"How could you know?" he asked.

She fiddled with a strand of the wig, then brushed it away and forced a sheepish grin. "I can only remember the first part of directions, so I always ask someone else."

A droll smile spread beneath his mustache. "Yeah, my wife's like that too. Drives me crazy. Here, I'll fix you up like I do her." He sketched a map on the back of a Consolidated Atomic public relations brochure, with an X pinpointing the dispatcher's desk. Then he went over it again, checking to see that she had really gotten it this time.

When she finally drove off, her blouse was wet under each arm from nervous perspiration. Feeling light-headed, she had to brace herself on the wheel, but the people strolling the paths glanced at her without interest, more intrigued by the messenger boy jumping

curbs on roller skates. For the first time that morning
she relaxed a bit and permitted herself a little sense of
excitement. Things were going as well as could be expected. The friendly atmosphere seemed to promise
that no one would interfere with her plans.

As she passed through the gates of the inner security fence which surrounded the reactor center, the
young guard spared the van a quick look, then returned to the comics spread on the counter. Almost
feeling sorry for him, she wondered whether he would
lose his job when the theft was discovered—and
whether he would find another that accommodated
Doonesbury.

She parked near a loading dock and stole a glimpse
at the hotel roof, knowing that Phillip would be
watching for her. As a signal to him that all was well,
she smoothed her hair and headed up the steps of the
barn-like building with her eyes cast down to avoid
the curiosity of the men in the area.

Beyond the open doors in the gloomy dusk of a few
incandescent lamps hanging high above the concrete
floor, the cavernous space was filled with row upon
row of boxes, crates, and steel drums.

Quickly she made a survey. Off to the right a trio of
walls enclosed an office where a woman sat pecking
at a typewriter, her face kept blank as if not to mar her
delicate features with expression.

Right away Lisa started to panic. The predicted
three-tiered carts were nowhere to be seen. Searching
every nook, she ignored the dispatcher seated at a desk
between the boxes near the front and headed toward

the only other door, but stopped when she spotted the candy machines of the snack room, which she recognized from the floorplans.

Reluctantly she turned back as the dispatcher called out to her. He appeared to be in his forties, with gray hair like sheep's wool and distinct cords of tension in his neck. Engaged in a telephone call, he raised an eyebrow in silent query.

"Western Union." She handed him the telegram and retreated toward the door. She was slipping into a daze and had to remind herself that this was not a dry run, that it was now or never. Her hands were clammy in her pockets; the lint stuck to her fingertips, forming little wet balls as she tried to calculate a delaying tactic.

Outside, a worker wearing a Dodger's jacket nicked a truck with the tip of a forklift, and the driver yelled at him with joking abuse. Hearing their laughter and awaiting the shouts of alarm that would be coming soon, Lisa felt as if a fist were squeezing her heart: Phillip had been in position for three minutes.

Squinting to adjust to the gloom of the interior, she suddenly yielded to a rush of relief as she spotted the carts hidden in shadows by the front door. There they were, treated with the same lazy abandon and casual disregard for security that Phillip had sworn she would find.

With a quiet smile she turned back. The dispatcher was puzzling over the message.

"Oh!" She put her hand to her mouth. "I forgot to tell you it's collect."

"Not for me it isn't. Looks like Emery Trucking literally got their wires crossed. It's a tracer acknowledgment for lobsters."

She took the cable with a look of embarrassment. "Sorry about that. I'll see that it's cleared up." Pocketing the telegram, she took out some quarters. "Do you have change for the Coke machine?"

"Sure, only it's fifty cents a can."

With a good-natured shrug she went to the snack room and stationed herself in front of a candy machine, studying the selections for the sake of any passersby. The rubber cement was hanging loose from one of her fingertips like a sloughed snakeskin, and she wiped it on her skirt before pumping some change into the machine, weak with anticipation now that she was so close to her goal.

Halfway through a bag of M&M's, she heard a high-pitched gasp and leaned out the door to see the typist clicking past on three-inch heels that made her hobble. At the sight of Lisa the woman halted abruptly, her mouth open in confusion, not knowing whether to speak or scream.

"A man's going to jump from the roof!"

"Oh, my God," said Lisa. "I can't watch."

The woman eyed her dead-on, but refused to share her squeamishness. With a dismissive twitch of her shoulder she rushed outside.

The dispatcher had already disappeared, lured away by the growing noise in the yard. Making certain that she was alone, Lisa lingered beside a column of crates and scanned the cavern, then quickly backed up to the carts. Without hesitation she picked up a can from a top shelf, felt for the beads that marked one of the skirt's fourteen interior pockets, and dropped it inside. The bulge was lost in the loudness of the paisley pattern. But when she had pocketed six more cans, the weight pulled the waistband so tight that she had to breathe with shallow flutters of her upper chest.

Out of nowhere a man in a white lab coat suddenly appeared, looking personally offended by her skittishness as she leaped forward into the light.

"Where is everyone?" He was crisp and defensive, as if shunning blame for having spooked her.

With a wavering hand she pointed at the throng at the back fence and mumbled something about a suicide. For a moment he whitened and regarded her with alarmed concern, as if thinking the threat were hers. Then with a dawning of understanding he pivoted toward the yard and plunged down the steps to take charge.

Readying for immediate flight, her body flooded with adrenaline, but when she imagined facing Phillip empty-handed, her pride forced her to return to the cart. Deftly she pocketed the remaining cans, then teetered down the steps with the stiff self-consciousness of a person in a home movie. Leery that someone might notice her odd performance, she kept her hands at her sides and held onto the fabric of the skirt to relieve the dragging weight on the waistband's hook.

The young guard was standing beside his booth, squinting in the direction of the faintly audible police sirens that became louder by the moment. Lisa shuffled to the van and climbed inside, the cans crashing around her knees, toppling her forward. As she struggled to regain her balance, the waistband's hook popped open, making the slide of the zipper bite into her blouse.

With deadly calm she tried to inch the slide over the cotton-matted teeth, knowing that she would never be able to drive with the bulk of the cans trapped around her knees and thighs. Finally, in desperation, she split the seam all the way down and dropped the loaded skirt around her ankles. Without bothering to put on her jeans she crept up to the driver's seat in her bikini underpants and backed the van out of the parking space.

Up above, Phillip was waving his arms and swaying on the ledge to elicit gasps from the crowd at the fence, like an actor in a one-reel comedy. With affectionate reproach Lisa thought how corny he was when he had an audience.

The ledge was just big enough to accommodate suicidal leapers of all sizes. It stopped half-an-inch short of his big toes, and the twelve-story drop to the sidewalk below made the blood in his vessels coagulate into cool mush. The clamor from the crowds in front of the hotel and at the fence floated up to him like diffused smoke, with new puffs of alarm arising each time he waggled a limb. Immediately after each of his efforts he tested the knot of the safety rope tied around his waist beneath his sweat shirt.

Back on the roof the door rattled as someone tried to force it open. Phillip pressed his arms rigidly along the wall, then turned his head to check that the heavy lag bolts he had driven into the door frame were holding fast.

Through the wood drifted a man's soft consolations. "Don't jump. . . . Let's talk about it. . . ." After a pause his sweet lilt continued. "Do you know that Jesus loves you?"

Giddy with tension, Phillip wavered between laughter and tears. He had spied a fire truck roaring out of the haze down the road, snatches of its sirens carrying on the wind. It lumbered to a halt in front of the hotel, and the crowd parted for the men as they leapt to the ground and rampaged up the lobby steps in a blaze of yellow slickers. Fleetingly Phillip wondered whether Lisa had gotten through the outer gates. Even though he was now beyond caring, he performed a final, wild display of losing his balance. Then, satisfied that he had done his best, he climbed over the railing, untied the rope, and raced across the sunroof. Just as he had anticipated, the pool was deserted. The guests had declined the amusement of swimming for the entertainment of a suicide.

Heavy firemen's boots stormed up the steps to the roof as Phillip looped the rope around the support of a guard rail, doubling it up. He snapped a mountaineering carabiner through the knot at his waist and back around the free length. Acting by rote, all fear and hesitancy disappearing in a surge of sudden clarity, he calmly stepped over the side and slid in a smooth descent to a balcony marked by a bright towel.

Feeling the solid concrete beneath his feet, he released one end of the rope and jerked it clear of the roof, then quickly stepped into the hotel room as the men up above succeeded in forcing the lags on the door, sending it crashing against the wall with a bang.

Shaken by the drop, Phillip sank to the bed and allowed himself a few minutes rest before rising to wash off the skin bronzer. Taking his time, he removed a small suitcase from the closet and changed into a dark blue, three-piece business suit, then packed the case with the wig, clothes, and rope. After leaving a tip for the maid who had been tending the room the past three days, he headed down the hall, but abruptly stopped to avoid a collision with the fireman who came barreling out the elevator doors.

"Are we on fire?" Phillip demanded.

The fireman checked the halls. "Did you see a dark guy in jeans and sweat shirt? About six feet tall with black hair."

Phillip shook his head. "Sorry, I can't help."

The fireman rushed toward the stairwell, and Phillip permitted himself a small smile as he took the elevator down to the lobby. Briskly he strolled out front where the crowd was speculating on his fate, keeping its position in front of the hotel like an audience which hopes to coax out a performer for an encore.

Pushing through the throng, he cut around to the rear of the shopping center and saw with relief that the van was parked behind the Baskin-Robbins.

Lisa was showing remarkable élan in having gotten herself an ice-cream cone during her wait, but he knew her well enough to spot the anxiety in her eyes.

"Terrific show, hotshot." She complimented him with a grin as he climbed into the passenger seat. She was wearing her jeans and immediately he turned to the rear where the skirt lay in a crumpled heap. He was almost afraid to ask.

"How many?"

"Why all of them, of course." Her eyes were abnormally bright. "Isn't that what I went in for?"

But the brightness suddenly faded. Her lids fluttered erratically, and the cone fell to her lap as she slumped over against the seat.

TWO

It was a day to draw the most reclusive Angeleno out of doors, the sky blown free of grime, the Pacific Ocean visible miles away, clear down Wilshire Boulevard. Unobscured by haze, the palm trees appeared shorter than usual; the buildings, closer together; the various parts of the city, actually connected. And on the hills of Bel-Air people gazed out in wonder to see the nearness of downtown, the shielding of the Bonaventure towers glinting like defiant swords drawn against the return of smog. All in all it was the sort of day residents cherished, one that permitted their sprawling city a relative intimacy.

Two at a time John Mezzantia bounded up the steps of the Federal Building in West Los Angeles, clearing the wide concrete slabs that were meant to guarantee a dignified procession. The building itself was a white, oblong monument to stability, and in a high, aerial shot it could easily have been mistaken for a tombstone. Inside the double doors he aimed a balled-up cigarette pack at an ashtray and missed.

Ignoring a glance of reprimand from a dour guard,

he jogged to catch a waiting elevator, and as it began to rise he felt as always the quiet anticipation of returning to work. Inertia seemed to drag everyday concerns out through the soles of his feet, abandoning them at the ground level.

On the seventeenth floor he pushed through the doors of the FBI's Los Angeles field office and noticed with chagrin that the furniture of the reception room had been reupholstered in a peach-and-blue floral print like that of a cheap movie lounge. Behind the plastic-laminate counter a woman wearing a dictaphone headset had her nose up to the carriage of her typewriter to align a form, but after fiercely striking a few keys, she ripped out the paper, smashed it into a ball, and tossed it into a scattering of similar balls on the desk. Petulantly she rolled in another sheet, then looked up at John as if daring him to comment, seemingly eager to transfer her irritation to an animate object.

"Mr. Kaplan has been asking for you," she scolded. "You're late."

"So I see." Like everyone else in the office he was resigned to suffering her presence for another week. After twenty-three years of dutiful service to the bureau she had abruptly given notice and lined up a job selling advertising space for a radio station. But meanwhile she had lowered the barricades on two-and-a-half decades of repressed resentment and was engaging in a policy of revengeful inefficiency that bordered on sabotage.

Scowling, she welded her smashed balls into a single globe which she aimed at a wastebasket across the room, sinking it on the first shot. In a smug glance she hailed her triumph.

He dared a request. "Any coffee left?"

"One cup." She walked to the urn, filled an earthenware mug, and majestically returned to her desk. Leaning back in her chair, she put up her feet and took a slow deliberate sip.

"I'm not into the submission thing anymore," she explained.

Too surprised to be offended, he regarded her with puzzlement, then turned and strolled down the brightly lit hall, trying not to breathe too deeply because the noisome odor of the cleaning fluid that the maintenance men used on the floors was particularly strong this morning. The offices of the assistant director were in the middle of the row, and John knocked perfunctorily before entering.

Edward Kaplan acknowledged his presence with a vague wave of the hand but remained absorbed in the uppermost layer of papers obscuring the blotter, his dark eyes and round brow impassive. He was an unabashedly plain man who early on had turned his appearance to advantage as a hallmark of stolid respectability.

Without giving the slight a second thought John settled into a chair in front of the desk, content to be ignored. Missing from a corner of the room was the beanbag chair that Kaplan had acquired a month before after taking up Transcendental Meditation at his daughter's suggestion. He had been motivated not by the promise of serenity, but by the possibility of quieting an embarrassing appetite that had given rise over the years to a large spare tire around his gut. The beanbag had been used for his noon meditations, but rumors that the New York office saw TM as disreputably avant-garde had begun to circulate, so apparently the beanbag had been thrown out and the weight left to flounder.

Abruptly, Kaplan looked up with an expression of surprise, as if not having expected that John would still be there.

"Well, John. How are you?" Not a rhetorical question, he expected an honest response.

"Fine, sir."

"What happened to your hair, for crissakes?"

"I had it trimmed."

"I guess you did. Looks like he used a chain saw."

"It was a she. With sewing scissors."

Kaplan chuckled and rubbed a hand over his face in a gesture of fatigue. "Seen any movies lately?" A dyed-in-the-wool Angeleno, Kaplan used films as readily as the weather for a stock lead-in.

"Nothing particularly memorable."

"Well, I saw a good one last night. One of those moody French adulteries. Short on story, but very visual. Cobblestone villages; bicycles and cows in the streets. I think you'd like it."

"I don't know, sir. Your track record's not so hot."

"When did I ever recommend a film you didn't like?"

"What about that ballet melodrama?"

"You didn't like that?"

"Not much."

"You're too hard-boiled, John. Tearjerkers are good for the soul."

John smiled and laid a folder of his recent reports on the desk. With a sigh brought on by the necessity of being serious Kaplan began to thumb through the sheets, periodically murmuring obscure approval or disagreement while twisting a finger in his ear as if to coax an olive from a bottle.

"Got anything on that Security Pacific case?"

John winced. The case was impossible, and accordingly he had been ignoring it. All over the Westside a well-dressed kid was walking into banks and politely demanding the money in the tills, never showing any sort of weapon and immediately leaving when confronted with resistance. But more often than not he was walking out loaded and had collected over thirty thousand dollars in the past month.

"No, sir. I've been concentrating on the Mary Rose Stoval case."

Kaplan frowned without apparent recognition. "Brief me again."

"That woman who escaped from the federal facility in San Diego by impersonating a male guard. She weighed about two hundred pounds, so it hid her figure pretty much, and she shaved her head and faked a mustache."

"Oh, yeah. Wasn't she in for something bizarre?"

"Murder by a technicality." As John crossed his leg, he noticed a hole in his sock and without thinking about it began to pick at the threads until he had uncovered his entire ankle, then stuck his foot under the chair. "Mary Rose had a history of impersonation and was doing pretty well as a general practitioner with phony credentials. But the prosecutor claimed it was negligence when a mailman she had treated for dog bite died of rabies. So the *practicing-medicine-without-a-license* charge became a felony, and the death was automatically considered murder."

Kaplan rolled a pencil across the desk, pressed for time but routinely interested. "You've come up with something new?"

"A tip that Stoval may be connected with a woman in Venice. A Lisa Ferro."

"Does this Ferro have a record?"

"Nothing. She's unemployed. Twenty-eight years old. Seems to be a drifter. I've been working it undercover. She thinks I'm a small-time drug dealer."

Kaplan flipped through the sheets with a sigh, as if indulging John in a more shallow lead than he had expected. He paused over a recent shot of Lisa at the beach, her lovely auburn hair billowed out like the wings of a gull, her eyes flashing in a sideways glance that seemed to generate electrical currents. John had snapped it under the guise of taking some scenic shots after she had refused to pose for him. But seeing it there in the file like a mug shot for identification, he felt a twinge of regret over the necessary deception.

"Pretty girl." Kaplan set the photo aside with a curious glance at John and then paused over a photo of Mary Rose Stoval, a three-year-old driver's license picture from the Department of Motor Vehicles. The black hair was a frizzy mane; the eyebrows, a heavy slash; the thick makeup, a mask to hide an obese face.

"Christ, they're beauty and the beast." Kaplan closed the folder. "So what do you think now? Is this Ferro woman the type to hide an escaped felon?"

"I don't know; she's defensive—and very cagey. I have a feeling she might be up to something."

"How ominous."

John ignored it. "I think at least it's worth pursuing a bit longer."

Kaplan shot him a dry look. "Is this pursuit aimed at laying her as well?"

"No, sir." He cleared his throat.

The pen lay barely within Kaplan's reach. He picked it up and tossed it into a ceramic jar as if to mark a break in tone. "Okay, go ahead with it. The other thing I wanted to mention is that we got a call from one of the physicists over at the RAM Corp think tank. He says he knows something about a uranium disappearance out at Consolidated Atomic. Seems like a touchy guy, but apparently he has a good impression of you from your investigation over there a few months ago, so I thought I'd let you question him. He'll be coming in tomorrow."

John nodded. "Has CA reported the material stolen?"

"Hell, no," Kaplan scoffed. "They're always losing track of that stuff. Their security isn't worth a crap. I don't know how many times they've been cited, so they're not going to be eager to admit that they were standing around with their dicks in their hands when someone waltzed out with the stuff."

"How much is missing?"

"Enough that I'd be scared stiff if I really thought it was gone."

"Maybe it'll turn up in a broom closet."

Kaplan smiled ruefully. "I rather doubt we'll get that lucky."

THREE

Lisa Ferro tossed the book to the end of the couch where it landed with a satisfying *thunk*, stirring up a little eddy of dust that annoyed her with its reproach to her housekeeping. For over an hour she had been studying a single page on ñuclear cross sections, but she knew that if she were to try to compose a one-sentence summary, even the first word would escape her, so it seemed utterly idiotic for her to keep pumping along like a dumb hamster going nowhere in a treadmill.

Screw it, she decided at last. *Let Phillip handle the technical side*. Physics was like some weird foreign language that she couldn't decipher even with a dictionary. Her job had been to get the uranium; Phillip could refine the damn stuff. Wryly she smiled at the notion of herself as the breadwinner and Phillip as the cook. She was feeling particularly in control today; the terror of CA, once gotten through, was exhilarating, and she couldn't help but feel a kind of cocky triumph over having put to shame all the staid forces of law and order that were designed to keep people like her in place.

Checking her watch, she saw that plenty of time remained before meeting Phillip for lunch at Farmer's Market in West Hollywood, and she decided that one little bag of cheese crisps wouldn't dampen her appetite too much. Her stomach could survive any patchy appeasements, but she couldn't find the damn Cheetos anywhere in the kitchen. The room was a godawful mess and so at odds with Phillip's green-and-white, copper-potted glory that she considered it a kindness of fate that he wasn't stopping by to pick her up today. For a moment she toyed with the idea of giving it a good cleaning, but as she looked around for somewhere to begin, the prospect began to make her groggy, and she abandoned it without a qualm.

Surveying the grocery sacks by the refrigerator, she saw that she had been too hasty in tossing garbage into them as they were not fully unpacked. Gingerly, she pushed aside banana peels and empty cans to pull from the bottom a six-pack of Coors and a bag of Cheetos, which she tore open with her teeth. Then grimacing in disgust at the rancid taste of the cellophane, she spat into the sink a bit of slime from an old cantaloupe. Really, she was becoming too slovenly even for her own low standards.

In a sudden burst of concern for hygiene she rinsed her mouth and decided that a beer might be just the proper antiseptic. With the end of a nail file she opened a push-top Coors can and swished the overflow off the counter into the sink.

Flopping back on the couch, she lay sipping at the beer, limited to the tiny swallows which she could manage prone, until a knock at the door startled her into spilling a warm splash down her neck.

"Who is it?"

"Me—" came a muted answer through the door.

She sighed and checked out the living room, kicking the textbook under the couch and shoving a roll of Phillip's drawings into the closet, while an impatient rattle of knuckles tried to hurry her along.

"Hold on! I'm not leaving," she yelled as she set about undoing the series of six locks. Finally swinging the door open, she faced Michael Greer standing in the hall. His sandy brown hair showed no sign of recovering from the impulsive trim with a sewing scissors she had given him a few days before, leaving the top hairs decently long but the sides badly botched.

"Well, can't I come in?" he asked.

"You look like Hitler," she said affably. "And no, you can't come in, because I'm going out to lunch."

He ignored her and came in anyway. She turned her back, walked to her closet, and rummaged for something warmer than her T-shirt, pulling out an old turtleneck she liked to wear when she was feeling reclusive. That and an oversized pair of sunglasses.

He sat on the couch and looked around expectantly with an energy for socializing that rather endeared him to her, against her better judgment. If any of his tales were to be believed, clothed as they were in grandiose exaggeration, even his biggest schemes were penny ante concoctions in comparison with what she and Phillip had in the works. And his indiscretion promised trouble.

He sipped at the can of beer, making a face of disgust. "God, how can you drink it warm like this?"

"Same as cold. Suck and swallow." She dropped the sweater on the chair and took a handful of Cheetos, feeling cheated that most of the crunchiness had been lost to the cantaloupe juice seepage.

"I called you a couple times. Where've you been?" His tone took for granted his right to know.

"Here and there."

"Are you avoiding me?"

"Apparently not very successfully." She proffered the bag, but he shook his head in refusal. "Did you know that you have a distinctive knock? You sound like the law."

As if tickled by a backhanded compliment, he reached up and pulled her into his lap, but she wiggled free, and he jerked away the bag. "How can you eat such garbage?"

"These're the organic kind." She licked the orange coating off her fingers.

After surveying the list of ingredients he scoffed, "They're a chemistry set. I'd never put anything into my body that I couldn't even pronounce."

"*Chee-tos,*" she said, prompting a reluctant smile. He had lain back on the couch as if bedding down for the night, and his study of her was intimate enough to make her melt. Why did he attract her so? Really, he was a waste of time, a worn-out, sixties hippy, overextended on credit for his spontaneity.

"Who're you having lunch with?" he asked.

"Just a friend." She decided not to mention Farmer's

Market, because he was a very vocal and missionary vegetarian and would try to tag along to browse the produce stands. And being the mooch that he was, he would probably end up borrowing money from her to buy turnip greens or some such crap. Never, in the short time she had known him, had she seen him eat anything except an odious concoction of raw vegetables, sprouts, and nuts. Spotting a corner of the physics book jutting from the couch, she kicked it back under, then sank into an opposing chair, almost enjoying the visit now that she took stock of herself and realized that she looked rather well today, her hair freshly washed and falling in soft auburn swirls around her shoulders, her jeans still tight from the dryer and unstrained because she had finally managed to lose the six pounds that had been nagging her all month.

Without any pretense at decorum he had picked up an old Rolodex of telephone numbers and started to flip through them, pausing whenever his interest was engaged.

"Make yourself at home," she said dryly. "I suppose you've already checked out my medicine cabinet and mail?"

Casually he replaced the index, but with a breeziness that suggested he was bored rather than reproved. "Do you happen to know anyone who would like to make some big money fast?"

"How fast?"

"Overnight. On the red-eye flight to New York."

Annoyed, she refused to answer for a moment. What made him think that she or anyone she knew would be interested in running drugs? Did she seem so petty and common that she would hire herself out for a job that any fool with a suitcase could do as well?

"No, Michael. No friends."

"No one who's hard up and doesn't mind a little risk this side of the law? There's a lot of money in it."

She sighed. Had the man no vision at all? She felt insulted by his appeal to the profit motive, as if he had never realized that she was attracted by the color and drama of experience in itself.

"No, I don't know anyone."

He accepted this with equanimity if not without a little skepticism, then he patted a cushion of the couch. "Come on, sit down."

Momentarily she wavered. "Really, I have to get ready."

"Are you by chance having lunch with another man?"

"Never mind."

"No, tell me."

"Oh, Michael, don't you ever stop prying?" Her tone was bantering, but inwardly she remained annoyed. "Why do you always make me feel as if I'm flat on my back with my feet in the stirrups for an examination?"

"Obviously I hit a sore spot. I don't suppose you're sleeping with him, too?"

"Oh, screw off, Michael. Spare me your insecurity." She plucked up the sweater. "I have a date, remember?"

"I hope you realize you're promiscuous?"

"Don't worry, I don't put anyone into my body I can't pronounce." Purposefully she strode into the bathroom and undressed, then turned up the water full force, wrapped a towel around her hair, and stepped into the shower stall. But as she soaped her body, she realized she had made a tactical error—he would figure that he could stay until she came out, and by then her anger would have softened.

The shower door snapped, and she ran her face under the water to rinse the soap from her eyes, then looked up to see Michael standing naked on the shower mat, smiling an apology as he moved into the stall.

"So you're promiscuous . . ." he said. "There are worse flaws."

"You realize, of course, that on that very long list of mine you can never hope to be anywhere near the top?" She was caving in to the jerk and knew it. But he was so beautiful nude; thin, tanned, and hard, with a chest of hair that seemed to cry out for soaping.

Already he was working on her with a bar of Ivory, so she picked up a bottle of shampoo and did what she could for him.

Carrying a tray of strudel, roast beef, and coffee, Lisa moved through the crowded patio that was the common dining area for all the food handouts at Farmer's Market. This complex of patio restaurants and wooden grocery stands had the air of having been erected on the spot by farmers who harvested with the rising sun to haul their produce in from the country. In fact most of the vegetables had been trucked down in semis from the San Joaquin Valley to Los

Angeles's Market Street where the vendors shopped in company with the buyers from Safeway.

She was boiling in her turtleneck sweater. Would she never learn to listen to the radio before dressing? The weather out her apartment window, which was shaded by other buildings and ocean breezes, never seemed to change, so she always dressed for the previous day. Yesterday had been overcast and cool, but today, with the typical inconsistency of a California winter, the temperature was hovering in the eighties.

A busboy finished clearing a table in the shade of a tree and she headed straight for it, annoyed to see a pair of teen-agers rushing to beat her. Without acknowledging their competition she held her tray aloft and took a shortcut by slipping sideways between racks of avocados, dropping into one of the chairs like a base runner sliding onto the plate and looking up at the boys with a victor's dapper satisfaction.

She spotted Phillip across the patio and felt the quieting effect that his presence always had on her, like a sedative that lowered her defenses and permitted a calmer vision. When she caught his eye, he acknowledged the distance between them with a smile that made her feel suddenly transparent. She was afraid that by looking at her face he could immediately detect her infidelity with Michael.

His hair was windblown, his skin still carrying a summer's tan, and his eyes were calm with the searching abstractness of a man who assumes the world will bend to his logic, and with the confidence that the logic is backed by something stronger.

Bearing a loaded tray, he was working his way around a group of Japanese tourists at the adjacent table who were filming one another eating lunch. With impromptu boldness one of the women aimed her movie camera his way to capture a few frames of a handsome American as casually as she would focus on a hula dancer or spear-throwing native.

Caught off guard, he gave the woman a bewildered frown, then automatically checked with Lisa, looking both embarrassed and somewhat pleased at being found attractive. But the moment he sat down, she sensed that he had something else on his mind and that he was holding it in check. He unloaded his tray with careful restraint and avoided her eyes as if assuming that she could guess the source of his concern.

Her pulse picked up; her stomach knotted with tension, and she busied herself by arranging the dishes. In broken Spanish she asked a Mexican busboy for water and offered one of the glasses to Phillip.

"You look like you need a drink."

"I tried calling you from the office," he said.

"I was in the shower." A fresh twinge of guilt at the deception. "So what's up?"

He stared at his lasagna as if it were medicine. "I'm worried about you."

"Oh, for crissakes, I'm fine."

"You frightened me yesterday."

"Why? Because I was a little unsettled for a moment?"

"You *fainted*."

"So?" Busily she began to cut up her meat to divert

his attention to the business of eating, but he wasn't buying.

"It would be perfectly normal for you to be so frightened that—"

"Well, we both know I'm not normal."

He ignored her asperity and after a few glances at the next table lowered his voice to hushed tones. His anticipation seemed obsessively controlled and his hands were squared into fists. "You know that once we start, we're not stopping until we succeed?"

The acidic pressure under her breastbone felt as if it might dissolve her down to nothing. Silently she pushed away the plate that was fogging under a layer of congealing gravy, and escaped his gaze by rummaging through her purse, seizing upon an unwrapped piece of gum that had picked up a dusting of lint. Delicately she picked off the fuzzy corners and put the rest of the stick in her mouth, giving it a few hard chews to get it started, then nervously cracking some inside bubbles against her cheek.

"So when do we get back to work?" Her self-assurance was a charade, but almost immediately she felt better. Where the fear had been, she experienced a pleasant numbness, as if she had swallowed a vial of liquid anesthetic.

"You look doubtful." His voice was steady with challenge, wary of forcing any enthusiasm.

"No, just cautious."

"There'll be risk."

"Calculated, I hope."

"As well as possible." His mask began to lift; his

eyes emptied of reserve and began to glow with an excitement that she could tell had been there all along. He was starting to smile like a sly adolescent about to take on an authority.

"You aren't afraid?" he asked.

She gave him a knowing, sidelong look, not yet as confident as he, but beginning to surrender to the lure of danger. "Isn't a little fear really the whole point?"

The rambling redwood house was set back on a verdant lot in the Benedict Canyon section of Beverly Hills. Its overhanging roof and projecting terraces gave it a clean, Oriental look and created an aura of security by sandwiching the occupants between seemingly inviolable barriers. The interior of the attached garage had been converted to a workshop. Five feet of raised oak flooring skirted the walls around a central parking area, which was flooded with an eerie, bluish glare from the fluorescent fixtures.

Pausing in a casual survey, Lisa examined a cutglass punch bowl coated with a hardened residue of glue which held a forgotten paintbrush welded at its center. Ruined Wedgwood bowls, crystal boxes, and silver utensils were scattered at random among the paint buckets and wooden stirring sticks, as if Phillip were totally indifferent to his wealth except that it spared him emergency trips to the hardware store when he ran short of tools or containers.

"I see you've been busy," she said.

He nodded and peeled away a long strip of masking tape, wadded it into a sticky ball, and tossed it over his head onto the paint-spattered drop cloths covering the drill press and lathe against the wall. A newspaper edged in beige dropped away from the glass and chrome of the General Motors van, floating over a final coat of airbrushed enamel.

"What do you think?" he asked.

"Gorgeous." She checked to see that the coverage was sufficient and that the old Western Union logo was obliterated. "Where did you stash the cans?"

"In a minute." He lifted a pan of liquefied solder from a hot plate and poured it into a silicone rubber mold. The mold had been taken from a stolen license plate, modified so that it couldn't be traced. Its numbers had been separated with a hacksaw, rearranged on a piece of plywood, and the seams smoothed over with wax.

As a layer of cooling gray dust floated to the surface, she recoiled from the acrid odor. "God, that stinks."

"I like it; it reminds me of peeling rubber in my first car."

She wrinkled her nose. "It reminds me of something more intimate."

He plunged the filled mold into a bucket of cold water, turned the mold upside down, and flipped out the new, solder license plate. After airbrushing it a bright blue he ran a roller of yellow paint across the raised numerals and print.

"Perfect," he decided.

"At least you'll be ready for work in a prison plate shop if things don't work out."

"I'm not worried." He opened a cupboard and removed one of the six cans of uranium oxide from Consolidated Atomic. But as he lifted the lid, she backed off.

"It can't hurt you," he said. "It's not radioactive enough."

Cautiously approaching, she studied the fine brown powder with awe. "How much?"

"About forty kilograms. It looks like we'll get a couple kilotons."

A grin crept over her face. She was leery of taking him too seriously and being made a fool for her gullibility, but the possibilities were intoxicating.

"We could split the whole fucking world!"

He raised an eyebrow. "Don't forget it'll take some tricky designing just to bring down the three million yards of concrete."

"But the damage will still be incredible!"

"A three-hundred-mile range with the secondary effects. If we wanted, we could go into the area after the blast. In Hiroshima the people who went in afterward were fine."

His eyes invited her to share his excitement, but she knew better. He always charged her with talking expectations into the ground, so she kept her speculations to herself. Although she would never admit it to him, she liked to think of the two of them as a new breed of terrorist, the first to get in synch with the eighties and own up to their hunger for power in itself, shunning causes altogether and finding motivation within themselves—the *me generation* of terrorists as opposed to *radical chic*.

Phillip replaced the lid and shoved the can back on

the shelf. "Let's quit. I'll start routing the neutron shield tomorrow."

She smiled and wrapped her arms around his waist, leaning her head on his shoulder. Her voice was soft and provocative. "Now what?"

He pivoted her around and held her tightly against him as if taking her prisoner, assuming the interrogating tone he always used when discussing their work.

"You *do* remember what a neutron shield is, don't you?" he asked as if it were a prerequisite to any further intimacy between them.

"No," she said. "But you're right. I should study more." Moving behind his desk which was piled high with journals, books, and pamphlets, she picked up a book and glided up the stairs to the old servant's quarters above the garage. The tiny child's bedroom was furnished with maple bunk beds bearing wagonwheels at the head and foot. The quilted bedspreads were printed with cattlebrands and the sheets with Roy Rogers and Dale Evans. The lampshade was a cluster of colored plastic balloons which cast a lovely glow of subdued pastels. It was a pleasant, cozy place to which they retreated when Phillip's capacious beige-on-beige bedroom seemed too open.

Lisa lay on her stomach with her bottom provocatively arched. Her eyes were studiously fixed on the page, but her mind was attuned to Phillip's first touch.

"Get away," she said when he came into the room.

He snatched the book and dropped it on the floor. Crouching over her as if to confine her, he kept his weight on his knees. "Okay, if you want, we'll discuss *The Curve of Binding Energy*."

Pulling off her slacks and blouse, he slipped a finger in the leg of her underpants and worked it slowly down between her legs until he found her slit. Gently he moved his finger in circles.

Pressing into the mattress, she reached up an arm to find the band of his jeans, but he pushed away her hand.

"Let's hear about mass equivalence and equations of state." He wrapped her hair around his hand, then bent to kiss the hollow of her neck, and she twisted beneath his knees and scooted down so that she could undo his zipper and tug off his pants. Urgently she worked his shorts down over his hips, and his erect penis swung free.

Delicately she kissed the tip, then held it in her hand and lightly squeezed as she kissed the projections of his pelvic bones and the smooth flatness of his stomach. She loved the salty taste and clean scent of his skin.

Taking hold of her wrists, he held them tightly above her head as he kissed her ears and breasts and the sensitive flesh under her arms. He removed her underpants and kicked off his own.

"I think I missed your answers." He took off his shirt.

"Be quiet." Gently she cupped his testicles and guided his penis inside her, feeling faint with pleasure at the first sliding contact. Her moans were soft and continuous, a coaxing language of appreciation and encouragement which rose in intensity with his thrusts until he paused to prolong their pleasure and they lay clinging dreamily to each other, damp and feverish.

He sat back on his knees, and his hand wound down between her legs, caressing her with a light butterfly brush of his fingertips as she set the tempo with the undulations of her hips.

Arching and stiffening, she drew all of herself to some imagined center, pulling in the varied strands of delight and holding fast until all were taut, and then in unison they snapped, their raw ends whipping free while her heels dug into the mattress. She cried out again and again, grabbing his hips and pulling him deeply within her, until the sharp pangs of joy had faded and she lay gasping for breath.

He withdrew from her, unspent, and lay back on the pillows. She rose to her knees above him and slid down over his erection, then bent to kiss his mouth, a deep, probing kiss that she could feel all the way to her crotch.

Slowly she moved up and down, supporting her weight on her arms, leaning forward so that he could take her nipples into his mouth while he cupped her breasts. Picking up the pace, she arched back and watched his hands go rigid around her rib cage, his mouth open with the pain of pleasure that was her power over him. Fiercely he gripped her, pressing her into his groin with such force that it hurt, and she bit her lip and moaned with the thrill of his release, then eased down on top of his chest to savor the quiet moment before they would part.

FOUR

The apartment walls weren't thick enough to muffle the sound of a good sneeze, so despite the forty-six degrees outside, the noisy air conditioner was running full blast for camouflage. Stifling a shiver, John was grateful when Colleen scooted to the bottom of the bed for the linens they had kicked to the floor. He watched the light from the open door fall along the curves of her back, over the long swirls of her hair, and down the slim roundness of her hips as she bent to retrieve a blanket.

With a sigh he floated on the edge of sleep, his body spent and soothed, and then the mattress shook as she pushed a pillow against the wall and fumbled on the bedside table for the lighter. Her cigarette smoke coiled around him, seeping into his lungs as if to prime them for conversation. From the corner of her eye she checked to see if he was dozing, and she extended the cigarette to him with a look of deep contentment.

"You know, I've been thinking . . ." She paused a moment to give him time to shift gears. "With your experience and my terrific dramatic skill I bet we could collaborate on something. Maybe a series about a crusader-rebel type of agent." She rushed her words together as if jammed for air time, but her eyes had all the time in the world, and he felt stroked by their gaze.

A rebel agent, he thought. *A contradiction in terms.*

"So what do you think?" She turned on her side and propped her head on an elbow. He smiled at her earnestness. She was an assistant professor of English at UCLA, moonlighting during her sabbatical as a bartender, with pie-in-the-sky aspirations of turning out some snappy, free-lance television scripts before she went back to teaching.

She blew a smoke ring and waved a draft to carry it aloft, the heavy lobe of her breast moving with the rhythm of her arm, then swelling attractively under pressure of an elbow brought to her side.

"Well?"

"Uh huh," he said, closing his eyes.

"Just the routine stuff, you know? The human side. None of the flashy murders or whatever."

He opened his eyes. "Flashy murders are cop stuff."

"Really?" She seemed intrigued by this, thinking it some inside bit of information. "What's FBI stuff?"

"Well, let me see. . . . This morning, for example, I tracked down a violator of the unsafe-refrigerator act."

"Come on, be serious." She fanned her hand to disperse the smoke, then absently stroked his hip, sending him bouncing straight up off the bed.

"Jesus, that tickles!" He tucked the blanket around himself like a protective wrapping, and she gave him a rueful smile. "Anyway, it's true," he said. *"It is unlawful to introduce into interstate commerce any household refrigerator unless it is equipped with a device enabling its doors to be opened from the inside."*

"God, that's an episode right there."

"The big cases are more exciting. I'm tracking down a kid for using the Red Cross emblem to solicit handouts—and a transvestite for impersonating a Wac officer."

"Ah, the pressures! I can see you're gonna be a candidate for heart failure long before you retire."

A strand of her hair had come loose, and he wound it around his finger like a silken tassel. "Only if you leave."

Her eyes swelled with surprise and she pressed her face down against his neck. He held her tight and breathed in the distinctive salty musk of her skin, a smell of ocean and freshly cut grass.

The doorbell rang. She shot him a questioning glance.

"I'm not home," he said.

"It's okay if you want to answer. I've got to go to work anyway."

"Already?"

She checked the clock on the nightstand. "Yep. Unfortunately. But if you come in later, I'll ply you with free drinks while we shoot the bull on some more of this G-man stuff, okay?"

Jumping out of bed, she considerately held a hand over herself to stem the flow of semen to the carpet, then shut herself up in the bathroom.

He smiled, threw on some jeans, and went to answer the door. The porch light had burned out, but in the dim glow of the living room lamp he studied the man in the wool herringbone suit, trying to place the azure eyes that seemed to pin one to the wall, the slash of handsome, ageless mouth.

"John Mezzantia?" the man asked, extending a hand.

The voice brought it back. The rapier-like thrust, brusque and full of a dark energy that commanded response.

"Dr. Lewis!" Immediately he regretted the exclamation, which revealed his relief over remembering the name.

"Are you free?" He seemed overwrought and kept looking around John to see if anyone else was in the room.

"Sure, come on in."

Lewis hesitated, as if resisting being drawn in precipitously. He seemed uncertain that he had calculated correctly in coming at all, but finally shouldered his large form through the door.

John settled him in an armchair and excused himself to return to the bedroom. Colleen had just finished dressing, and he held a finger to his lips, raised a window, and silently mouthed, "Out."

"Who is it?" she mouthed back, her face alive with the prospect of intrigue.

"No one." He had learned long ago that if a man was on the brink of informing, as he suspected Lewis might be, the introduction of a third party could bring on immediate constraint and ruin any hope of getting information. Six months ago, when Lewis had called the bureau from the RAM Corp think tank, where he was employed as a nuclear expert, he had reported leaks of his own classified work, which concerned the possibilities of producing atomic explosions from the low-purity uranium products in the nuclear fuel cycle. The bureau's subsequent investigation had failed to pinpoint the source. But John had always vaguely wondered whether Lewis hadn't leaked the stuff himself to prompt tightening of security at the fuel processing centers, then called in the bureau as an afterthought to protect his own security clearance. Prior to working for RAM Corp Lewis had designed atomic weapons for the government, but had quietly been urged to leave when he began publicly protesting the declassification of top secret atomic research for the use of the reactor industry. Gradually becoming more radical in his view of the dangers of homemade nuclear bombs, he had become a regular speaker at antinuclear demonstrations and on university campuses.

It occurred to John that in wanting to discuss the uranium missing at Consolidated, Lewis might be hoping to make restitution for the leaks—or to take credit for his foresight in having predicted that such a disappearance was inevitable.

Colleen pointed at the bedroom door and indicated that she wanted to listen, holding a hand over her mouth in a vow of silence, her eyes pleading complicity. But when John took hold of her to throw her out, she squirmed free and climbed out the window alone, then stood in the bushes with an ear cocked in his direction, miming eavesdropping.

Grinning malevolently, he shut the window and closed the drapes. To cover his delay he flushed the toilet, slipped on a shirt, and returned to the living room. Lewis was looking at *Playboy* and appeared to have relaxed somewhat.

"How about a drink?" John opened a liquor cabinet to encourage acceptance. *Get them high to get them talking.*

"Uh—just water." A cautious man.

John handed him a glass and took a seat on the couch. He caught Lewis's eyes scanning the modest furnishings, the sharp appraisal making him acutely aware of the room's aesthetic shortcomings. In his expensive hand-tailored suit and soft Italian loafers Lewis looked decidedly out of place. Apparently physicists earned more than John had supposed.

"Was there some reason you didn't want to come in to the bureau tomorrow?" asked John.

"I thought this would be more relaxed." Lewis leaned anxiously forward, looking anything but relaxed, and speaking with a kind of compulsive directness. "At the FBI I'd feel about as useless as a textbook in a reactor meltdown."

John chuckled, trying to spark rapport. "Half the time there I feel like that myself."

As if rejecting an indifferent wine, Lewis set the glass of water on the table. "I suppose your people talked to ERDA about that uranium out at Consolidated Atomic?"

"Of course. Who told you about it?"

"It was inevitable that someday the shit would hit the fan." His eyebrows lifted in challenge, an absurd attempt to dispel the abstractness of the think tank and to claim more prescience than the bureau. "And

they told you no problem—right? That it'd take another Manhattan Project to build a bomb with stolen
uranium?"

"Who says *stolen*?"

"What else?"

"Maybe just misplaced. In the fifties an entire atomic bomb was thrown out on a garbage dump with
some scrap casings. It could have happened to the
uranium—or maybe it never even existed. Consolidated keeps telling us that bookkeeping errors happen
all the time." He watched Lewis's eyes flare at the
indifference, and he knew that he had taken the right
tack. Nothing made an informer more careless than
scornful skepticism. "You know, usually the colorful
explanations aren't worth a crap. I always start out expecting the obvious. Simple solutions seem to work
best."

"That oxide disappeared from a move cart. I've seen
them myself, loaded down with enough fissile material for two or three bombs, sitting on an open-air
dock. It just takes one nut who decides he's got a better use for that stuff."

"One nut and a million dollars and a retinue of experts," said John. Obviously the guy knew more than
he was telling; he seemed to be seething with a private fire. Was he worried that his lectures had inspired the theft, and was he trying to mitigate his
guilt by calling in the bureau as he had done before?
But to all appearances Lewis was far removed from
any guilt. He stared at John as if he were a turtle on
the road to be run over for sport.

"Look—" He seemed to fumble for a polite alternative to *asshole* but gave it up. "If I had those cans of U-235 tonight, I could go home and make a bomb with enough yield to bring down both ARCO towers and to wipe out most of downtown."

"I think you'd be out of a job if you couldn't. You were a bomb designer after all."

"So it doesn't worry you that there might be a psycho out there who's trying to graduate from dynamite pipe bombs to the real thing? Maybe you don't realize how technically crude a successful bomb could be. It doesn't take an Oppenheimer anymore. College kids have designed some that would definitely work."

There it was again, thought John, that look of snotty superiority, almost a note of defiance. The guy seemed ready to explode. John found himself wondering if, just as many firemen were repressed pyromaniacs at heart, many bomb designers weren't repressed terrorists who had channeled their aggression into government service.

"Why do you keep suspecting a psycho?" asked John. "Doesn't it seem more likely that if the stuff was stolen, it was taken by a foreign government or international terrorist?"

"We're talking about forty kilograms, for crissakes! That's a flash in the pan. Governments wouldn't bother with it and neither would terrorists. The PLO and IRA couldn't afford to use a nuclear weapon and make the whole world side against them."

John fiddled with an olive pit he had found in a button well of the couch cushion, speculating whether scientists weren't driven to paranoiac assumptions just to abate the boredom of their dull research. Perhaps

Lewis lost sleep over all the other half-baked conspiracy theories of assassination and corporate collusion.

The doorbell rang, and Lewis's eyes glazed over at the interruption. He sat on the edge of the chair and straightened his suit jacket as if preparing to leave should John's attention be diverted for any length of time.

John opened the door to find Colleen staring at him with sudden timidity, jerking her hand away from the bell as if caught in a prank.

"You okay?" she whispered dramatically, as if she had returned only to check on his safety.

"No, my life is hanging by a thread. I suppose you're armed to the teeth?"

She peered over his shoulder, trying to catch a glimpse of his visitor by standing on her toes and craning her neck. Projecting for the benefit of the audience within, she said, "Did I forget my purse here?"

He gave her a stoney look, then allowed the door to swing closed and went to the bathroom to get the purse from the shelf, feeling not at all amused by her cunning in having left it behind. But when he returned to the door, she was gone.

Lewis was leaning back in his chair, hands folded on top of his head in an attitude of boredom. He jerked his head toward the kitchen door. "In there."

She was waiting for him in an alcove between the stove and refrigerator, entrenched beneath the spice rack. "I really did need my apartment key. I wouldn't have bothered you otherwise. . . . I even tried the window first."

"Uh huh."

"But now that I'm here . . ." She shrugged, the tenor of the gesture sublimely hopeful.

"No."

"You could introduce me as another agent?"

He shook his head. "This is ridiculous, Colleen—you don't even know what we're talking about. It's not the adventure you think."

"You've got an informer in there, right?"

"Wrong. No informer, no spies, and no criminals."

"Then why not? There are woman agents, aren't there?"

He opened the back door onto a little walkway. "You can't sit in. It's against regulation, and that's that."

"Since when did you care about rules?"

Putting an arm around her shoulder, he started to pry her out. "Look, this is nothing that would even interest you. I'm getting rid of the guy."

"Then why can't I stay?"

"I thought you had a job."

"I've been late before." There was a lilt of pleading in her voice suffused with so much desire and energy that he felt his resolve oozing away like warm honey.

"Will you keep your mouth shut?"

"Totally shut. I'll even breathe through my nose."

He sighed and preceded her into the living room. As he introduced her to Dr. Lewis, he ascribed to her a vague connection to the bureau. But rather than spooking Lewis into diffidence as John had feared, she seemed to impress him as a potentially more sympathetic audience, making him lean forward and embroil her with his blazing eyes.

"Are you on the Consolidated case?"

She hesitated a moment, then shook her head and shot John a proud glance which demanded credit for not having opened her mouth.

Lewis eyed her with curiosity, then gave the slightest nod of acceptance, as if one game more or less were irrelevant to him. With a calm gaze, as if deciding to be reasonable and patient this time around, he turned to John.

"Do you know why I quit designing weapons?"

Hesitating a moment, John debated whether to go along with this lowering of the guard. "I got the impression you were eased out for making waves."

"I forced the issue. I wanted to leave. The standard of quality was maximum destruction—I had to lie about my work or be a social outcast. It was like being an executioner: if I talked about it, everyone despised me."

"I get that in my work sometimes."

Lewis shook his head, refusing the comparison. "It's not the same. Creativity in the service of death—do you know what that does to you? You start thinking of yourself as a monster and wondering if you're still human. The responsibility is horrifying—if you do your job well, it can mean the destruction of humanity. But pretty soon you start hoping that one of the damn things will actually be used—or you've been working for nothing. You want to see if they'll blow up something besides an underground test site. Lots of my colleagues were dying to use nukes during the Vietnam war because they wanted their babies to make a public debut."

John rose to refill their glasses, then sat clinking his ice for a moment. He felt an easing of tensions and leaned forward in response, but was careful not to be lulled from his skepticism.

"So now you're worried that some nut might feel the same impulses?"

Lewis's nod was almost defiantly frank. "I can understand how someone with problems could become obsessive about controlling that sort of power. I've seen it myself. People become fixated on packing more and more power into smaller and smaller packages. I used to devour the results on destructive radii, always aiming for larger fireballs and more compressive force. It was a heady game until I'd hint at my success to someone on the outside and be shunned like a madman. With Three Mile Island part of me was hoping for a meltdown, because I knew that a disaster was the only thing that would wake everyone up and get us out of the nuclear mess."

John felt his doubt beginning to subside and had to force himself into the role of adversary—although part of him wanted to set aside professional objectivity and explore the incredible possibilities.

"Are you still hoping for a disaster?"

In a way that despaired of John's ever getting the point, Lewis sighed. "It just scares the hell out of me to think there might be someone out there who can't hold himself back. Stealing weapons-grade uranium seems to point to that."

With a jerk of understanding Colleen started forward in her chair. "Someone stole uranium?"

As a reminder of her vow of silence John gave her a reproachful glare. "This is all speculation, Colleen."

"But uranium! Jesus Christ! What will they do with it?" She turned to Lewis, who looked satisfied—almost soothed—by her wild reaction.

"I sort of doubt they'll use it in a homemade nuclear reactor," he said dryly.

"Do you know who took it?"

"No, almost anyone could have known the move carts weren't well guarded."

On the surface of Lewis's smooth theorizing John detected the merest ripple of subsurface churnings. "You didn't just *happen* to mention something about those carts in one of your lectures, did you?"

The placid reserve visibly bubbled, showing widening circles of anxiety. "Uh . . . unfortunately I believe I have," said Lewis. "From time to time."

"Jesus Christ . . ." Colleen whispered again to the room at large. "Could they really build an atomic bomb?"

FIVE

In the wake of an afternoon shower a wet-basement odor hung over Westwood Village and seemed to drip from the boulevard trees. Raindrops on the leaves refracted sunlight into bright starbursts; brick-fronted shops reopened their doors; pedestrians discarded the sodden *Herald Examiners* that had served as impromptu umbrellas, though the more timid among them still fended off the sky as if wary of the sudden clemency.

John Mezzantia sidestepped a puddle on Weyburn Avenue and hoped that the break in the rain would last the afternoon. He had popped a seam in the shoulder of his raincoat, and his suit jacket was wet to the skin. He sighed over a bumper sticker on the back of a pickup truck mounted with steer horns on the hood, parked in front of United Western Arms. It read: *I'll Turn In My Guns Over My Cold Dead Body*. Why in hell, he wondered, did the bureau give him every piddling job in the Village?

Bracing himself for a confrontation, he pushed through the doors which were backed by heavy steel bars and looked like the front of a cage designed to restrain the brute behind the counter. The man dwarfed John's five feet, eleven inches and outweighed the shop's brass cannon. Around his gargantuan hips in a superfluous display of power was strapped a Colt Detective Special.

Waiting on a couple of smart-ass kids who listened with mock deference, the man was giving a pitch on an antique Smith and Wesson that he claimed had been used by Bill Cody on a buffalo hunt, but the kids kept exchanging grins and finally one of them erupted into laughter.

"You talking about the Bill Cody who pumps gas over at the ARCO on Wilshire?"

With a disgruntled wag of his head the man returned the old pistol to its case, then turned his attention to John, lifting an eyebrow in a silent query.

"I'm looking for a gun."

"We don't sell groceries." An automatic response, flattened by countless repetitions. The man's accent was Louisianian or Mississippian, laced with a nonplussed hostility from decades of waiting on people. He followed John down a row of cases but kept looking back at the kids. They wore hooded UCLA sweat shirts and kept their hands in the pockets as they examined a tray of old bullets.

Most of the guns were antiques, tastefully displayed on swatches of worn leather, woodburned with Western scenes.

"Do they have to be registered?" asked John.

"Mister, you gotta register everything these days," the man drawled, establishing himself as one of those Southerners who become more Southern the farther they drift from the South. And then he snapped his head around to catch one of the boys sliding a cartridge up his sweat-shirt sleeve.

"Leave that!" His voice split the air like a swinging axe. "Less you two pissants plan on shittin' them bullets tomorrow morning."

The kid let the bullet clink back into the tray and tried to cover his fear with bravado by mocking the accent. "Horse turds."

His friend giggled, but upon drawing the owner's glare, withered and skulked toward the door, closely followed by his defiant companion. They exited with a burst of laughter so loud and chafing that it sounded more like a bray of terror.

"Low lifes," the man muttered. He hitched up his holster and looked around for agreement. John nodded vaguely while examining a pistol in a velvet-lined box equipped with a barrel that was well over a foot long.

The man opened the case with a key from his belt and extracted the gun. "This one here'd shoot the butt off a bee at ten yards."

"Exactly what I wanted it for," said John, the levity falling flat as the man scrutinized him, blank-faced. Admiring the intricate scrolls and vines engraved in the metal, he aimed the gun at a little girl holding a fishing pole on the cover of a sporting magazine. The pearl grip was inset on both sides with five-pointed silver stars, and he felt almost tempted to buy the thing.

"That's a beauty, ain't it?" asked the man. "A Buntline Special. There's a legend that Ned Buntline gave five of these long-barreled Colts to Dodge City law-men like Wyatt Earp and Bat Masterson. I traced this one through the Colt records before the fire burned up their invoices a few years back. It was a presentation piece for a Texas senator in the late nineteen hundreds."

"Nice. How much?"

As if anticipating his demurral, the man smiled and flipped the lid to reveal the price sticker of $2,200.

"Oh, well . . ." John set it down and pulled out his credentials case to show his badge. "I didn't want to talk while the boys were here. I believe you called us?"

The man examined the badge as if trying to decide whether to stock up on a gross for the shop. "That was a couple of days ago. Boy, you sure do take your time in coming! It wasn't me who called, it was my son." He sounded proud, then shook his head and explained, "It's not everyone who'd take the time to help you boys out. He'll be back soon—he went out for some lunch."

John lost himself in a survey of the guns, disappointed at not being able to summon up the fierce cravings of his boyhood now that he could afford to satisfy his impulses. As a sort of present to the little kid who had idolized Hopalong Cassidy he bought himself a tiny replica of a six-shooter and amused himself by firing off miniature caps until the front door opened and the son returned.

He appeared to be in his early twenties and wore a meticulous white shirt and gray slacks but had neglected to shave the sparse chin fuzz that made him look like a sloppy eater of cotton candy. He carried a paper plate covered with aluminum foil, and when he set it on the counter, his father made a hasty introduction. Having done his duty, the owner tore off the foil to reveal neat mounds of the same ham hocks and limas that John had had for lunch at Westwood Drug. Primly he took a taste with a plastic spoon and without giving John a parting glance he retreated quickly to some back room, like an animal dragging its kill to its lair.

The boy watched him go with a look of tolerant amusement, then turned to John. "I suppose you've read a report of my telephone call."

"How about going over it again."

"But I thought I heard recording sounds on the phone!" His smugness was that of a student hoping for a compliment on an astute observation. "Don't you record all the calls?"

"Only the important ones." An irresistible cheap shot.

With a blink the boy laid the Buntline in its box and locked it under the counter, the action an apparent comment on rudeness. But he was willing to rise above it and fixed a look of cooperation on his face.

"On last Tuesday . . ." he paused for reflection, as if to get his facts exactly right ". . . a young woman came into the shop and started asking questions about whether we could get her something we didn't normally stock, hinting that she'd pay handsomely for it. At first I inferred that she wanted an M-16 or silencer or machine gun—we do get requests for those sometimes. But then it developed that she wanted a bazooka!"

Inwardly John groaned. Why was he always turned off by these helpful types? The kid revolted him for some reason. "The bureau is only concerned with firearms cases when there's a suspicion of spying or terrorism. Otherwise, you'd want to speak with the Bureau of Alcohol, Tobacco, and Firearms, or the local police. The legality of bazookas is a state matter."

"She *might* be a terrorist! Who knows? When I tried to get her name, she told me there were other fish in the sea and stormed out! She was the snotty type—you know. Thought that just because she was pretty, she could wrap me around her little finger."

Oh God, thought John, *the people who call the FBI whenever they feel insulted!* Was the Bureau supposed to track down the girl and charge her with snottiness? But dutifully he asked a few questions, getting a report of the conversation and a description of the woman. It was the easiest way. He had learned never to contradict people's self-importance; if a crank told him that his landlady was a communist because she subscribed to *Redbook*, he would promise to investigate.

When he finally extricated himself from the boy's cloying theories, it was nearly one o'clock. The sky was clearing, and it looked as if the break in the rain would last the afternoon. He considered stopping by his apartment just to touch base—to drop off his umbrella, check the mail, and use his own bathroom. The day was a bust anyway; nothing was panning out. He had reported the substance of last evening's conversation with Dr. Lewis, but had been told by the agents who were working the case that in spite of some strange circumstances surrounding a suicide attempt at the Malibu Sands Hotel, the top executives at Consolidated Atomic were refusing to concede that a theft of uranium had been committed—undoubtedly because the admission would send bushels of heads rolling down CA's flowered drives.

A young man in soiled corduroy pants slunk out of Ye Corner Doughnut Shoppe, holding onto a paper cup which disappeared beneath the bill of his yachting cap with each delicate sip. As he passed John, he unfolded an imperious palm. "Have you any spare change?"

John dug for some coins and avoided the dead, flat eyes. The kid was part of the coterie of Village crazies, an outpatient of the VA hospital who engaged his own store window reflection in arguments about the merits of various old films, lapsing into the dialogue of the female characters.

"Thank you kindly." The kid pocketed the coins with a carefree flippancy which meant that John had been played for a sucker—a pathetic salvage job on dignity that John could accept.

A cool breeze rattled loose some stray raindrops from the leaves, and John pulled up the collar of his coat, feeling suddenly melancholy as he jaywalked across Weyburn and then Gayley, ignoring the indignant horns that greeted his passing. Defiantly he looked around for the Village's infamous motorcycle cops who roared after wayward pedestrians like round-up cowboys, all but wrestling people to the pavement and hog-tying their hands and feet. He had always dreaded being stopped by one of those leatherbound morons and forced to show his badge, detesting his affiliation with them as *lawmen*. But today was not the day. Two at a time he took the flagstone steps up to his building, which was set atop a slope overlooking the Village. His apartment was on the first story with an exterior entrance. Initially he had planned to move into a second-story unit in the same building, but had worried about the lack of privacy. Compulsively curious himself, he imagined that any downstairs neighbor would be equally nosey, snickering knowingly every time his bedframe squeaked and he and a girlfriend padded to the shower, so he had waited for vacancy on the ground level.

He dug out his ring of keys.

"Hey, Mike!" A woman's shout sailed up from the bottom of the steps, and he looked around before it occurred to him that he was being hailed by his alias. He swore at his suit, which screamed "*fed*" loud and clear, and just managed to yank off his tie before Lisa Ferro's face appeared over the top step. She was panting heavily. "Jesus, you need a rope tow here!" She raised an eyebrow at his outfit. "What'd you do—join a fraternity?"

"Look, don't screw this up for me, okay?" He stepped away from the door and lowered his voice to a whisper. "The apartment belongs to . . . a friend. A business friend. Understand?"

"Not really." She was taking in the ivied arbor over the porch and the pots of bougainvillea, but he hooked her arm and was relieved that she submitted to being led past the mailboxes, taking an obvious inventory of the names as they went back down the steps.

Once on the sidewalk he suppressed his concern and forced a show of indignation. "Would you mind telling me what the hell you're doing here?"

"I saw you walking by, so I followed."

"What are you doing in the Village?"

"Shopping." She opened a Bullock's bag to show a stylish navy-blue sweat suit. "Like it?"

He smiled at its innocence. "Let's get out of here."

As they walked to the corner, he reviewed his afternoon wanderings, wondering at what point she had started to follow him, feeling professionally embarrassed at not knowing whether he had done anything to arouse her suspicions. His visit to the gun shop had been in character, but his straight clothing was a real giveaway. At a Greek falafel handout he ordered coffee while Lisa eyed the tubs of mashed peppers and sesame seed paste.

She pressed an elbow into his side and nodded at some purplish mush that the counterboy was spooning into a pita bread. "You honest to God eat that bird-food?"

"Sometimes," he hedged. Had she seen him scarfing ham hocks at the drug store? Mike Greer the avowed vegetarian?

They sat in a redwood booth, and he leaned back against the wall, admiring the plasticized canopy that diffused the light like dark stained glass into a sepulchral glow. "I sure as hell hope no one saw you through a window back there. Or you've screwed up a coke buy I've been arranging for weeks. I bought this suit just because they won't let you near the place unless you look as straight as a law professor."

"Sorry." She finished stirring a third packet of sugar into her coffee. "I wanted you to help me with a job tonight."

"Doing what?"

Fiddling with the stir-stick, she wedged it between a slot in the table's boards and drew it back as if cocking a slingshot. "Nothing much. Drive into an alley, get up on the roof of your van, and cut a cable."

"Which alley do you have in mind?"

"Pontius, in the industrial part. The cable comes off a pole, then spans the alley for about thirty feet. It's simple."

He waited for her to continue. "I assume this line goes somewhere . . . ?"

"Yeah—Western Patrol."

An inane grin crept over his face. Western Patrol handled more than half the silent alarms for all of Beverly Hills, Bel-Air, and Brentwood. Despite the evidence to the contrary he had never really believed Lisa capable of anything criminal, and yet facing it now, he felt a strange stir of excitement—a lawman's fascination with the exoticism of the outlaw.

"Don't you think it's a bit grandiose to knock out the security for a couple hundred estates?"

"So? I'm not looking to get canonized."

"Western Patrol will know right away that their main line is cut."

"And what are they going to do about it?" She took

a sip from her cup. "It'll take them hours to phone their entire list of clients and then dispatch patrol cars to the places that don't answer. And by that time I'll be home having coffee."

"How many of the houses do you think you'll get into?"

"One."

For a minute he thought that she was making fun of him—that she'd burst out laughing and get him to admit that she had really had him going there for a while. But she kept a straight face.

"Why can't you just cut the line at the other end like everyone else?"

"Because in Beverly Hills the lines run underground. I can't get at the telephone lines—or anything else—until I'm inside."

He was stunned by her nerve—Lisa, with her lovely cheerleader's face and innocent halo of silken hair. It was as if his mother had just confessed to membership in the mob.

"What're you worried about?" she demanded.

"I think it's overkill, to say the least."

She made a moue of annoyance. "Burglars who play by the rules and don't waste protection get caught. Why should I give a shit if I break the cookie jar getting at the cookie I want?"

"Which is?"

"Never mind."

"I'm not part of this, Lisa, unless I know."

"Come on," she coaxed. "You don't really want to know. . . ."

"*Tell* me!"

"A bazooka." She was almost coy.

He looked at her wide-eyed, then reached across the table and laid a hand on her arm. "Lisa, I think you should go home and take a nap and forget about all this."

"Uh huh. Are you in or not? It's five hundred dollars."

"Who's in it with you?"

"No one."

"What's the target?"

She shook her head. "You don't need to know that. I've got the cable cutters in my car. Now is it yes or no?"

He nodded reluctantly. *Oh, yeah,* he thought, *it's yes, all right.*

SIX

The earth at the base of the scrub oak was torn in a narrow grave, snugly lined with a plastic tarpaulin that was invisible in the blackness. The night breeze made Phillip shiver as he surveyed his diggings, and he zipped up the jacket of his jogging suit. His stomach and gut were cramping so severely that he wondered if he had gotten food poisoning during Lisa's dinnertime rantings on the importance of a full stomach in keeping one's composure.

Silhouetted in the pale moonlight, Lisa held the shovel as stiff and reined-in as a sculpture, with her eyes frozen in warning against any suggestion of turning back. Catching his gaze, she shifted the shovel to the crook of her arm and pushed the button of her LED watch.

"It's time," she whispered. "He's cutting the cable."

Dolefully he started down the slope of the wooded Benedict canyon lot, keeping his focus on the light emanating from the estate ahead, wondering why on earth he had ever let her talk him into this.

Leaves and branches crunched underfoot as they made their way to the fence, where Lisa pulled equipment from her athletic bag with the determination of a kid who has spent years between Olympics getting ready for a final shot at a medal. She tossed him a ski mask and gloves, then threw a canvas tarp over the strands of barbed wire atop the chain link fence. By the light of a yellow bug lamp shining out across the estate's patio and pool he watched her nostrils flare as she jammed a toe of her tennis shoe into a hole between the wires and hoisted herself up.

Then abruptly she dropped back to the ground. "Mother fuck . . ."

His legs tingled with adrenaline, primed for flight, but as she turned around and switched on her penlight, he noticed that the seam of her pants had split from the waistband to the crotch. He sagged against a fence post, trying to cap the giddy laughter bubbling up within him. As if trying to weld the fabric together, she groped behind and squeezed the seam, releasing all her pent-up tension so intensely he was afraid she was going to cry.

"Hey, come on. It's not that bad," he said. But she stepped away from the fence and turned toward the hill, and he went after her. "What's the matter?"

"I have to go home and change."

He stifled the invectives that came so readily to mind. "Uh—Lisa, it's not really crucial that you look your best tonight."

"I'm not going in there feeling ridiculous!"

With all the calm he could muster, he removed his jacket, and she snatched it to tie around her waist by the arms, then patted herself down to make certain she was all neatly tucked out of view. Brusquely she returned to the fence, all self-assurance again, as if the pique had been a little farce to put him at ease. He could see only dimly in the darkness but knew that look in her eyes—the sternness of a teacher attempting to divest her students of any inkling that she would weaken again.

She pulled up on the fence and swung a leg over with natural agility, untouched by the dictums of girlish awkwardness. Then light as a cat she dropped to the other side and landed in a crouch. He tossed over the athletic bag, and her catch made a soft, cupping sound which was partially muffled by the scattered shrubs. Still, he waited to make certain the noise had not been detected before he climbed to the other side. With Lisa plucking at his sleeve, they treaded around the swimming pool where an inflated plastic goose was making a solitary sail toward an eerie glow that reminded him of vats of uranium rods, with the same sense of contained power.

At the patio's sliding glass door he balked over the sudden sight of his own reflection, an ominous black form in a sinister ski mask. Lisa caught her breath and poked a finger in his side to get his attention. Lifting the door in its frame, he eased it back the fraction of an inch the lock permitted while she inserted the end of a metal file and flipped the catch. Absently he made a note to install security bars in the tracks of his own sliding doors at home, thinking that there was no point in going through this twice, once as perpetrator and again as victim.

They tiptoed inside. The house was quiet. No creaking floorboards, no panicky breathing, no urgent phone calls. Illuminating her path with a penlight, Lisa padded to the basement to clip the telephone wires while Phillip stood guard at the kitchen table and tried not to worry about the reliability of the man she had hired to cut the alarm cable—nor the odds of their getting out alive.

When she returned, flashing a circle of thumb and finger to signal her success, they cased the first floor. It was all as he remembered it: tasteless baroque furniture, gilded and carved in rococo curlicues like the prizewinning efforts of a cake designer. Room after room of claw-footed couches, figurative clocks, velvet upholstery, and bronze nymphs—the bounty of the owner's twenty-year reign over an inherited hardware empire.

At the end of a vaulted hall Lisa stooped in front of a sculptured door and dug into the athletic bag to remove a sixteen-inch suzi, which she wrenched over the knob like a pair of pliers to silently break the lock.

The interior of the room was lined with glass-fronted cabinets which paraded row upon row of weapons. The history of each piece was detailed in skilled calligraphy on scrolls of parchment, a professional job which ignored the hand of the owner and made the place look like a public museum. A long case in the center of the room contained the more exotic items, including a medieval ball and chain, an engraved crossbow, and a collection of World War II memorabilia which was set up in a kind of macabre shrine with draped photos of Hitler hung over the case between a Nazi flag and a golden eagle emblem. A leatherbound, gilt-edged copy of *Mein Kampf* lay displayed in the manner of an open Bible, as if to snag converts to the faith.

"Gee, how nice," whispered Lisa. "Almost makes you wish the Krauts had won."

Failing to spot the bazooka in any of the cases, Phillip examined the walls and floor for hidden panels and loose tiles, then got down on hands and knees to check the cases for false bottoms. He found to his chagrin that the weapons were displayed directly on the baseboards.

"Are you sure he still has it?" she asked.

He shrugged. "Guess we'll have to wake them."

The prospect filled him with qualms, but Lisa was nonplussed. The sight of so many weapons had gone to her head and made her itch for action. She turned off the light, withdrew her pistol, and led the way from the room with a penlight.

At the staircase to the second floor he assumed the lead and ascended next to the wall, praying that the heavy Oriental carpet masked the creak of his ankle bones and knees. Did professional thieves limber up before starting out? Pausing at the first door of the upper hall, he flicked the light across a pair of Snoopy quilts harboring two small girls whom he guessed to be the owner's stepchildren. He had heard that the old man had remarried after the death of his wife, to a woman young enough to be his daughter.

Carefully, he checked out the other rooms on the floor, although the location of the master bedroom was obvious from the start. Raucous bursts of snoring marked it as effectively as a hawker outside a burlesque show.

Across the midline of the room's king-size bed the old man lay sprawled on his back, pushing aside his wife, who was curled into a fetal crescent with her knees pulled up to her waist. Apparently nude beneath the blankets, she appeared to be in her early thirties and had a face that retained a varnish of hardness even in sleep.

Lisa hit the switch of an overhead light, and the woman's arm jerked in reflex over her eyes, while the old man burrowed under a pillow until he rammed the headboard and buckled up his buttocks like the cars of a crashing train.

"Oh, for God's sake, Harold . . ." the woman lamented sluggishly, still drifting in sleep.

Lisa flipped back the blankets and sheet, and the man sat up all at once, lunging in confusion to recover the lost warmth and then reeling back as if jolted by a live wire. He tried to open his eyes, but was confounded by the sudden brightness, and he batted out with a hand, shadowboxing his fear and uttering a series of primitive growls. In the past twenty years he had aged forty; his naked gut hung to his genitals like a water-filled balloon that shook with each wild thrust.

The woman was awakening in response to her husband's activity but seemed to be fighting something with more pull than sleep, a leadenness dampening her movements like heavy casts on her limbs. When at last she managed to open her eyes, terror flamed only briefly before being quenched by an automatic cool, leaving her looking annoyed at having had her rest disturbed. Slim and heavy-breasted with long black hair that glinted bluish highlights, she lifted a perfectly manicured hand to her forehead, shading her eyes from the light, and gazed out at Phillip, looking wary and guarded but prepared to see what would happen next.

"Keep quiet and your kids will sleep through this," said Phillip, embarrassed by the gangster tones which tumbled so easily from his lips. Lisa had gone to the closet for some bathrobes, which she tossed onto the bed. The man grabbed up the one on top, oblivious to the ruffles at the neck and wrists as he jammed his arms into the tight sleeves and clutched at the folds in front for protection. His compulsive movements and the lack of focus in his eyes made Phillip wonder whether the man had imbibed before bed while his wife was popping her pills. With subdued irritation the woman had taken up the oversize man's robe and slipped into it, then submitted to handcuffs.

"We want your bazooka," said Lisa. But the man remained rigid and stoically silent, seemingly expecting some measure of respect for his defiance and challenging them to beat the information out of him, his die-hard masculinity still intact after all these years.

"The bazooka," Phillip repeated menacingly. And in drugged appraisal the woman narrowed her eyes.

"Fine with me." Her voice was calm with exploratory indifference. She looked over at her husband like a schoolgirl who had impulsively switched cliques and rejected an old friend as an initiation rite. But the callow meanness was overlaid with a mature bitterness that seemed to have festered with time. "Go ahead and take the damn thing."

"Where is it?"

After waiting for the man to answer, she sighed over his stubbornness, then swung her legs off the edge of the bed. She beckoned Phillip to her dressing table where she took a critical look in the mirror and wiped away mascara from under her eyes, her skin looking dead, a wan olive tone like waxed bronze.

"I said, where is it?" He watched her hands in fear that she would go for a hidden weapon.

"It's in his gun room. He'd keep me and the kids there if he thought we were important enough." She realigned her bangs with a finger that bore a diamond the size of her bottom front teeth, giving him a coy little smile which asked indulgence for female vanity. She seemed accustomed to handling men so long that the absurdity of reacting with allure toward a thief in a ski mask went right by her, although the calculation behind her flirtation was as blatant as the rattling of an adding machine. He knew the type, the ones who married for love only after they had accumulated fortunes from their first divorces. Undoubtedly she had a lover stashed in a Brentwood apartment awaiting the alimony.

"Let's go." He checked to see that Lisa could control the old sphinx in bed, then followed the woman downstairs to the vaulted hall. He noticed how lax she was about the sloppy lapels covering her ample breasts. At the gun room's open door she made a knowing sound, low in her throat, showing her admiration.

"I see that you're an expert in your work."

He inclined his head toward the door, and she

moved inside, leaning back on one of the cases like a woman with something on her mind.

"Could you do a little job for me?" she asked sweetly. "I have something special to give you if you can make it look like part of the break-in."

Confused by the proposition, he nibbled at the wool of the mask. "What do you mean?"

She tossed her head. "Haven't you ever killed anyone before?"

At first he didn't get it; he toyed with his pistol like an actor taking refuge in props while trying to recall his lines. And then the light dawned. "The old man. . . ."

"My *husband*—" She sounded offended by the reference to his age, "is dying anyway of a very painful disease."

"Yeah, old age."

She shrugged; she wasn't going to beg. "Take whatever you want here. Personally I've always thought that this collecting is pretty strange. My analyst says that guns are phallic and that my husband is probably a repressed fag. I don't know how you do these things, but if you need something that can't be traced . . ."

She pointed to a Mauser Broomhandle on the wall.

"Get the bazooka," he growled. Obligingly she got down on hands and knees to crawl under one of the cabinets. Delicately, she fiddled with something on the bottom as he crouched down to watch.

"Damn! I broke another nail, and I just had them done!" She sat up cross-legged and sullenly sucked at a fingertip. "God, that makes me mad; it's so expensive! I go to Mr. Bruce—he does Streisand. . . ."

Phillip swallowed uneasily; the woman was completely mad. And yet, down at this level he could see what she had been going after. There was a slight unevenness in the depth of the cabinet's two sides, as if it had been designed like a magician's box to make things disappear. Certainly it was reasonable that her husband had gone to such lengths for camouflage when possession of a bazooka carried a stiff fine and a prison sentence.

"Get me a knife," she said. She extended a flat palm, and then broke into laughter at his alarm while she jangled her handcuffs. "Oh, come on! Do you think the lady can filet you wearing these bracelets?"

He handed her a penknife and watched as she pressed the point of it against one of the wooden dowels, producing the sharp, metallic click of a releasing spring-loaded catch.

Heedless of her flopping robe, she used her coupled hands as a third leg to crawl from under the case. Smoothly she folded down its back, revealing a bazooka that was wedged into the triangular opening looking no more lethal than a Polish sausage.

A pulse of glee shot through him. He grasped the gun by the breech guard and muzzle and eased it out. It was still in excellent condition, just as it has been the first time he saw it more than twenty years ago. He remembered his longing and his awe, how he had been scorned back then as a scrawny, mousey child by the two inebriated adults—Phillip's father, the engineering magnate, and the owner of this house, flush with his new hardware inheritance. Boasting and showing off to each other, they had forgotten that he was there until he had sneaked out a tiny hand for a loving pat on the cold metal. The old man had begun to sober up then and had subtly threatened him about keeping the gun a secret.

But now it was his! And though he still felt sick with tension, he was pleased that Lisa's efforts to obtain a gun through more conventional channels had failed and that he had been forced to take this risk. Fondly he laid it on top of the glass and noticed that the barrel was flawless, well-oiled against corrosion.

The woman ignored the bazooka as if it were a common plumber's wrench. She chewed on her cracked nail and touched a finger to her tongue in the gesture of a smoker removing bits of tobacco. "You know, Harold may not look it, but he's a real screamer when he's hurt. So you really should gag him first, or the kids . . ."

Too much a lady to go into all the unpleasant details, she let it trail off, then blinked as another idea took hold. "And could you tie me up first, so the police will know I wasn't involved?"

"How about in bed?" He dropped the bazooka shells into the athletic bag. "Then you'd be fresh for tomorrow."

She turned down the corners of her mouth at the levity of his tone, but seemed to be giving some consideration to the content when she was suddenly distracted by the sound of running steps in the hall.

Breathless and anguished, Lisa leaned in the door. "There's a cop car out front!"

He slung the strap of the bazooka over his shoulder, and they tore through the house with the woman run-

ning after them, her shackled hands clasped to her
breast as if in prayer. At the kitchen door she blurted
out, "You're not leaving, are you? I can tell the cops I
tripped the alarm myself! And later I'll say you were
holding a gun on me!"

"Yes, do it." He caught Lisa's shocked eyes staring
through the holes of her mask as he pulled out a key
and unlocked the woman's handcuffs. "You realize
that it's your neck, too, if we get caught with this
bazooka?"

The woman nodded gravely. "I know."

"Then leave this door unlocked, and I'll be back later to do that job."

They sprinted into the yard, and he mounted
the fence and sat astraddle it while Lisa handed up
the weapon and bag, then climbed over to take them
from the other side. In the darkness they made their
way up the wooded slope to the tall, silhouetted oak
which marked the open grave, and he laid the bazooka
to rest within the plastic shroud, then shoveled the
mounds of dirt on top while Lisa gathered loose
leaves and twigs like a creature possessed.

Without his jacket he was beginning to shiver, and
his discomfort aggravated his irritation over the
flunky she had picked as their accomplice. "Remind
me to hire an electrician the next time we need an
alarm cable cut."

For once she was wordless. With testy impatience
she jerked off her mask and patted down her hair,
looking every bit the Beverly Hills housewife ready to
jog off a few extra pounds in the night air.

Lights were going on throughout the house as they set off on their run, and Phillip found himself wondering when the woman would realize that he was not coming back. Would she call a locksmith to unhandcuff her husband from the bed? Surely she wouldn't wield a hacksaw herself and risk breaking another fingernail!

The agents and cops crawled around on the lawn like a gang of spiders at work on a cooperative web, jumpy with expectations of what they might trap. Watching from behind a clump of ice plant by the driveway, John calculated where he could hide if shots started flying, and he decided that he would be least vulnerable stretched out along the curb where he could justify his presence as the covering of an escape route.

Most of his fellow agents had heard rumors about the possibility of confronting a bazooka tonight and had managed to escape before assignments were made, so it was a small contingent which skittishly advanced to ring the bell. The door swung open, and immediately the men relaxed their tight formation to confront a woman of stunning beauty, her hair in wild disarray, her robe open on a cleavage which, even at a distance of fifty feet, took their breath away. She gave them a sleepy smile as she shook her head in response to their questions, balancing her weight on one slim leg while hooking a bare foot around in back. Eagerly the agents moved inside, though it seemed evident that this was a false alarm.

Strangely relieved that Lisa had not carried through with her crazy scheme, John felt certain that she would have been caught by the roadblocks set up to examine outbound vehicles. He checked the time to see whether he could still make it home for *The African Queen* on the late show, but found that his watch had finally succumbed to its accidental run through the washer and dryer in the pocket of his jacket.

Turning onto his back, he cushioned his head on the ice plant and was enchanted by its sweet odor as he tried to spot a star through Los Angeles's hazy canopy of night lights. With a smile he recalled his naiveté during his early days with the bureau when, bored with the routine of investigating applicants for government jobs, he had longed to take part in raids and arrests.

A sudden rustle of grass made him sit up with a start, and he watched the cops on the lawn dart around to the rear of the property while Kaplan, the assistant director of the L.A. office, charged a yucca plant from behind, waving his walkie-talkie in a mad signal for John to follow him to the front door.

Breathlessly he caught up. "Is Ferro here?"

Kaplan rushed inside, his fat buttocks lumbering from side to side like the backpacks of a mule. "We found an old man handcuffed to his bed."

In the entry hall the woman was surrounded by officers as she sat on the arm of the sofa, demurely holding closed the neck of her robe while staring at her lap with a sheepish smile. She sucked absently on a torn fingernail with unwitting sensuality, and John noticed more than one hand in a pocket to hold slacks away from an erection.

Curtly, Kaplan took one of his men aside. "What's her story?"

Stricken, the agent glanced back at the woman as if embarrassed to reveal a privileged intimacy. "She says the old man is her husband . . . and that he . . . uh, gets off on being bound while she, uh . . . does him."

SEVEN

Floating in his swimming pool, Phillip watched a few submerged leaves sway to the strokes of his hand in a delayed reaction. He felt calm and fulfilled by this morning's return trip to the hillside for the retrieval of the bazooka. Now the worst was over.

The muffled drone of a propeller airplane reminded him of the Los Angeles of his childhood, the sleepy stillness of suspended time. He loved the underwater quiet, the magic of total silence—a perfect antidote to the frenzied excitement of stealing the bazooka two nights before and slipping back this morning to unearth it. There were no pressuring voices here; nothing seemed urgent. He felt a quiet anticipation, a delicious readiness, as if he were a coiled snake ready to strike.

Hearing a splash, he looked up to see Lisa clambering up the pool ladder. He backkicked from under the diving board to see what was wrong.

"Are you all right?"

She shucked her scuba gear and squeezed the water from her rope of hair, then lay spread-eagled in the sun on the double chaise longue. "My ears hurt."

Disgruntled by her giving up, he removed his own gear and wondered why he had been stupid enough to waste a Sunday morning trying to teach her anything when she was in such a contrary mood. He hoisted his tanks to the pool's cement skirt and flopped beside her on the chaise, glancing uneasily at the upper windows of the neighboring house as Lisa unsnapped her bikini top and let it fall to the ground. In a nest of folded arms she cradled her head and sent pearls of water onto her tanned shoulders.

"Are you still brooding about that cable alarm?" he asked.

She rolled her head to look at him, her eyes wide with self-defense. Then she blinked an indifferent dismissal that put him on the other side.

"I never brood." She sounded manic, as if trying to alter the facts with intensity alone.

He wanted to pick her up and throw her back in the pool. "Let's go to the lab. I've got something there that'll cheer you up."

Listlessly she tagged along across the patio, her Beachcomber Bills slapping up and hitting her heels with a wet sucking sound.

The living room of the guest cottage had been converted to a small laboratory, the ceramic-tiled walls lined with Formica counters, vacuum outlets, and racks of reagents. The larger equipment—a fume hood, induction furnace, and glove box—was placed along the outer wall.

Over his swimming trunks Phillip pulled on a lab coat and filtering mask, experiencing as always the sense of official sanction the outfit bestowed, as if anything he might choose to do were beyond the limitations of moral concern. Lisa watched from a wheeled stool, and he found himself playing to her lack of understanding, making the procedures more recondite than necessary, using pipettes when graduated cylinders would suffice, putting watch glasses on all the beakers, and substituting tongs for fingers. He felt rather like a magician or priest, and he recalled his first enchantment with science as a kid when he had mixed bleach and ammonia in an improvised glove box and tested the resultant mustard gas on the pet hamsters he had received for his birthday.

Absently, he smiled as he emptied out a can of Consolidated Atomic uranium oxide onto a furnace tray which was mounted on spring legs and motorized by a probe through the wall to a hand vibrator.

Lisa picked up a burette and blew across the top of it, producing a single foghorn note. She nodded at the vibrator which was bolted to the counter. "When do I get it back?"

"Better buy another one."

"Uh uh. Too embarrassing. I got that one through the mail."

"So you're a prude at heart." He emptied the tray into a crucible, added potassium chlorate and magnesium, and ignited the mixture with a length of electrical cord which was stripped of insulation on one end, its circuit completed with a loop of resistance wire. After cooling the burned-out mixture with a spray of water, he knocked away the residue and regarded the resultant lump of fissionable, weapons-grade U-235 with exultant awe.

"So what did you want to show me?" From a bottle of mercury she poured a puddle into her palm and let a blob of it slip from her hand. On impact it split like a mitotic cell, with its duplicate silvery selves taking off down the counter.

He abandoned the lump of uranium; he knew his pleasure in it could not survive the weight of her funk, and instead he pointed out the hemicylindrical shells of the tamper which lay on the workbench like the halves of a large tin can split lengthwise. Together the halves would encase the uranium core and act as a bumper to reflect neutrons back into the chain reaction, countering their tendency to shoot away like billiard balls flying off a game table. The core would be fastened to the muzzle of the bazooka as a target, and a gunpowder charge would shoot a small, cylindrical uranium plug through a hole in the tamper into the hollow of the core, forming a critical mass upon detonation.

"Well, what do you think?" he asked.

"What're the chances of the whole thing being a dud?" Her voice was flat, as if daring to broach the unthinkable, but her eyes betrayed a mean satisfaction in challenging his prowess.

"None." An outrageous exaggeration.

Preoccupied with a pestle she had found, she ground it against the counter, leaving a deposit of crushed glass, then she threw it aside, suddenly possessed by an idea. Without a word she strode into the house and took a seat on the Herman Miller rolltop desk in his den, her wet bikini spreading a water stain on the walnut while she rifled through a Westside telephone book.

He placed a hand on the receiver when she reached for the phone. "Who're you calling?"

"A business friend of the jerkoff who was supposed to cut the cable."

"Maybe he didn't cut it because he was caught—"

"No way! I checked that alley three nights in a row. It was totally deserted." She dug at the dial with savage sweeps and gripped the receiver tightly until her look of sudden alertness revealed that the call had been answered on the other end. Remaining silent, she listened to a man's repeated *hello*, which was audible even to Phillip. After a moment she hung up and stared at him wide-eyed, as if facing a long-denied fear. "I think that son-of-a-bitch is a fucking fed."

"What're you talking about?"

Apparently absorbed with guilt for being taken in, she refused to explain.

"Does he know about me?" He felt a strange surge of excitement, a thrill at the possibilities of pursuit. But she shook her head in denial, and he felt compelled to extort assurances. "You're positive that we're safe here?"

"Yeah, we're safe. But he's not," she said. "Before this is over, I'm going to bring that bastard down!"

From a distance of several blocks John could hear the roar of the shore-breaking waves and smell their salty musk. He pushed up the collar of his turtleneck sweater against the ocean fog that rolled over the beaches and down the deserted residential streets.

The clapboard siding of the apartment building yielded a soft hollow for his spine as he leaned back against the wall and took a final drag on his cigarette, cupping his hand over the tip to hide the glow, then flipping the butt into the surrounding darkness. With deep breaths he tried to dispel his uneasiness about the job ahead, but his mind kept peeking around its blinders, debilitated by a vision of an acrobatic crossing to a window over a four-story drop.

It was a rotten night for breaking and entering. He doubted any evening would seem opportune, but the few times before he had pulled off black-bag jobs, he had experienced nothing like the weak-kneed fear of the common thief that he felt coming on tonight.

His feet hung free in space, and he swung them a little to pump the blood back into his ass, which had gone numb from hours of sitting on the sharp grating of the fire escape platform. At the end of the alley, four stories below his precarious steel perch, a couple of men were stealing lumber from a post office construction site. He wondered whether they would have the temerity to continue if they realized that a federal agent was observing them from above.

The truck pulled away when it was filled to capacity, and John warned himself against any further delay. Already the neighborhood was settling down. Soon people would be asleep, and accidental noise would be too conspicuous. He would have to begin while he could still count on the camouflaging cacophony of television programs, marital arguments, and flushing toilets.

Yet he still continued to wait.

Reluctantly, he had agreed to the necessity of planting a bug in Lisa's apartment, but he found himself resenting his orders to gain entrance in spite of six locks she had installed on her front door. If it had been his decision alone, he would have waited until she showed up again, and then risked going to her with an apology for his failure on the assumption that he had not yet blown his cover.

But the assistant director was more impatient for answers and had gone ahead and secured a court order for electronic surveillance.

John's destination was a partially opened bathroom window eight feet from the fire escape platform. A neighbor's bathroom window intervened, the two rooms having been built back to back on a common drain, and fortunately the neighbor showed no signs of being at home.

With pale determination he pulled in the fishing line tied to his wrist, holding it out beyond the platform's edge so that the attached rope, uncoiling below, would not snag on the way up. Grabbing the rope's tip, he threaded it over the railing and hauled up the bundle at its other end—a battered surfboard shrouded in black foam rubber. As if believing he had foreseen the usefulness of a strong and lightweight ramp for work at forty feet aloft, he congratulated himself on not having thrown it out when the newer, shorter boards came into fashion.

The fin prevented the loop from slipping off the tail as he eased it out toward Lisa's window while holding the rope taut to keep the board parallel with the ground. Twisting and maneuvering, he angled the fin over the sill and wedged the tail tightly against the window frame, securing the board's nose to the fire escape platform with screw clamps that countered its tendency to roll.

As he climbed over the railing, his palms were slimy on the bar, and his head pounded so wildly that he feared it would pitch him off to the left. With his arms raised like wings he edged one foot ahead of the other and took four cautious steps forward until he was able to touch the wall of the building with an outstretched hand. A seam in the clapboard promised to serve as a guide, and he grasped the tiny outcropping between thumb and forefinger as he waited for the courage to continue, his resolve beginning to crumble like a sand castle in a hot wind.

His stomach lurched as a switch suddenly clicked in the neighbor's bathroom and light flooded through the gossamer curtains onto the board. With her dress already raised to the waist a woman hurried through the door and sat on the toilet, turning her face toward the window as she reached for the roll of paper on the wall. Involuntarily John started and sent the board wobbling beneath his feet. In numb panic he shifted back over the center line, his gasps of despair drowned by a roaring flush that seemed to be a drumroll preamble to his fall into space.

In an instinctive grope for safety he splayed his hands flat along the building wall, unwilling to part contact with anything rooted to firm ground, even when the light had vanished at last. So with thumbs hopefully planted in a seam he shuffled sideways on the board until his fingertips bumped the projection of Lisa's window frame.

Crouching, he jammed a leg through the opening with sufficient force to chip the plaster and then locked his heel against the inside wall. He deftly worked in the other leg as he sweated in nervous triumph over fear and gravity. With the window lifted fully open he climbed inside and smiled foolishly at himself in the medicine cabinet mirror, pledging everlasting avoidance of anything as stupid as what he had just done.

In the living room he searched for a place to plant the bug, somewhere that Lisa would not be cleaning or dusting—although now that he looked closely, it appeared that she dusted nowhere at all.

As he checked behind a vivid horse blanket that was used as a tapestry above the couch, it occurred to him that considering Lisa's nature, the bedroom would be a better bet. He noticed that the rumpled sheets had not been changed since his last visit and wondered whether she had been staying away the past few days because she suspected that her apartment was being watched. *Was she with another man?*

The heater vent by the bed was an obvious choice. He removed the screws with a pocket knife and lifted off the grating, then stuck the bug to the back of the metal vent with a double-sided, spongy tape. The freedom to uninhibitedly explore her apartment intrigued him. He never tired of trying to piece someone's secrets into a revealing portrait. The fact that his snooping was officially sanctioned alleviated his guilt, but he knew that the bureau's interest in sending him here did not account for his willingness to pry once the problem of gaining entry had been solved.

Lisa's books were all paperback thrillers; her records were hard rock; her clothes appeared to be almost new, and there were no dresses at all. On her closet floor lay a wadded-up skirt that was torn up one side. The thing was incredibly ugly—paisley-printed and full enough to make a set of curtains. He couldn't believe she had ever worn it.

Almost nothing in her dresser was folded. Sunglasses, jewelry, and scarves were mixed at random. Her underwear drawer was full of practical cotton briefs and silky lingerie. He held a lacy black bikini up to the light, marveling at its lightness and smallness, imagining her in it.

Beneath the panties he found some snapshots of Lisa in the nude and felt a stab of jealousy over the photographer's shadow, which had been cast onto the bed where Lisa sat. She was clowning in a few of the shots, but in most she was looking straight into the lens, challenging it, oblivious to her nudity and confident of her appeal. There was no coyness to her poses; she was lounging about as she always did after making love.

From his pocket he took a Minox camera to copy them for inclusion in her bureau file. According to regulation he should insert them as they stood, but he knew that he wouldn't. He felt too protective of her. First he would crop them at the neck.

As he finished shooting, impulsively he pocketed one of the better pictures, because he knew the copies wouldn't be very good. She had her chin haughtily raised, obviously at the limit of her patience with the picture-taking session, but with the spark of energy and zest in her eyes that he so liked.

If she missed the photo at all, which he doubted, she would think he had taken it the last time he was here. Any man who knew her would want one.

By the light of the dashboard clock John checked the address; the house was not quite what he had expected for the home of the assistant director—something more austere and remote seemed in order. It was set in a development on the carved-out mesa of a mountain overlooking the ocean in Malibu, and the others on the street were identical in design, distinguished by a little balcony, a bit of brick facing, or a window box of marigolds.

Hours before he would not have believed that the worst was yet to come, but now he felt as if he were in a perpetual free fall in space, his only point of purchase the hope that Lisa's demented cohort of terrorists would fit the typical profile of ineptness.

He took up the envelope of photographs from the seat and started up the drive. It was well after midnight, but the entire household seemed to be awake. The argument of a young boy and girl carried clearly in the quiet of the night. His knock was answered by a tiny blond girl in a worn-out Superman costume that was so large for her, the tights hung in puddles around her feet. Without flinching at the sight of a strange man she moved aside for him to enter, as if thinking him a friend summoned over to join the fun. She was four years old at most, and he wondered what she was doing out of bed at this hour and how a man like Kaplan, with an administrator's requisite sense of order, could survive such a chaotic household. Strewn around the carpet like abandoned projects were toys, games, and a box of crayons—partially ground into the nap where someone had stepped on them.

"Is your daddy home?"

Solemnly she nodded, and rather than leave a scene of potential interest, she yelled for her father at top volume.

Through an archway to the living room a pair of Pekingese dogs were watching television while a teenaged girl lay curled on the couch, absorbed in a paperback with a bloody axe on its cover, apparently sharing her father's consuming interest in crime.

The children's argument was becoming more virulent as the girl threatened to split open her brother's head with a baseball bat. Suddenly the whole house shook as if a crate had been dropped, and the boy ran laughing past the entry hall landing, apparently having escaped his sister by jumping over the second-story railing onto the stairs. He gave John a quick glance, then disappeared to the lower level with a bang of a door and the shot of a sliding bolt securing his domestic safety.

From the end of the hall Edward Kaplan peered out a doorway. The stuffed pockets of his plaid Bermuda shorts made his hips appear half-a-foot broader, and his thin legs jutted from the hems like two golf clubs. Startled by the sight of John, he nodded at the envelope of photographs.

"Is something wrong?"

"I'd say so, sir."

The little girl had been watching for a reaction to their visitor; she pulled at her father's shorts, keying on his distress and looking up at John with eyes that mirrored her father's alarm. Diplomatically Kaplan sent her upstairs to search the pockets of his suits for loose change, then guided John back down the hall to the kitchen.

The room was neat and quiet, an obvious refuge. Containers of flour, sugar, and milk were open on the counter. Mrs. Kaplan sat on a stool, squinting at a black-and-white television set the size of a snapshot. She looked quizzically at John, clearly having forgotten their introductions at the bureau Christmas parties, but smiling with the ease of a lifelong friend.

"We were having a snack," explained Kaplan. "Want a waffle?"

"Uh—no thank you, sir."

In what looked like a game of competition, Mrs. Kaplan flipped open the lid of the steaming waffle iron and speared the first golden square. Her husband shot her an insider's glance that asserted she had had an unfair advantage with the distraction of company.

"Try one?" She slid the plate in front of John under a deluge of hot syrup, but the sight of the crunchy pockets made him feel nauseated with tension.

"Take that one and leave us alone, honey," Kaplan told her pleasantly.

As if used to being excluded from bureau business, she complied nonchalantly, and John wondered whether she would remember him the next time they met, but decided she wouldn't if the previous introductions had failed to take hold.

"So let's see what you've got." Kaplan stirred the bowl of batter in the crook of his arm as if cradling a baby while John set out the photographs he had taken of the various books and pamphets in Lisa's apartment, saving the worst for last. Periodically Kaplan bent down to look at one of the pictures, and the batter oozed to the edge of the bowl before he straightened and started stirring again. Finally satisfied, he brushed the iron with butter and poured on a little puddle.

"Well, obviously this looks like scary stuff," he said. "But it doesn't seem to indicate any real technical proficiency. Maybe she's only fascinated with the idea. Kids make designs all the time as a lark. A boy in Miami had everyone hyped up a few years ago with his A-bomb design."

"I'm afraid it's not that innocent this time." John set out the photograph of an architectural plan of Consolidated Atomic with the area of the loading dock circled in black.

"Oh, Christ . . ."

"I've called CA already, sir. And they tell me those plans have always been available to anyone through the Energy Research and Development Administration."

Kaplan stared past the photos into space. "It can't be coincidence that you were on her tail from the beginning. We don't get that lucky. Did you see any sign of that escaped psychopath she was supposed to be associated with?"

"No, nothing. But she can't be alone in this."

"That tip you got, what about it?"

"It's the key, but a dead end." The lab had ruled out any possibility of tracing the anonymous note linking Lisa Ferro to Mary Rose Stoval. John had found it stuck under his windshield wiper in the Federal Building parking lot a few months ago, and it had prompted him to begin an investigation by finagling an introduction to Lisa. The note was scrawled on a form taken from the post office and could have been left by anyone who had watched him enter the building.

John removed the final photos from the envelope, and Kaplan gazed down at them forlornly as the thick odor of burning waffles filled the room.

When smoke started to spill from the slit, John forked the charred mess into the garbage disposal and watched the sodden lumps melt under the swirling waters.

"So you think this is their target?" asked Kaplan.

"Maybe. I can't predict her. It seems totally insane, but . . ." He shrugged. But what? Did he still expect rationality from Lisa?

Impatiently Lisa watched their tiresome wrangling—the salesman, overbearing and determined to close the deal, and the husband, taciturn and doubting. The wife hung in the background with a tight smile of irrelevance on her lips as she slid a hand into her purse for one of the candies that she sucked like some vital drug. They stood among the cabin cruisers which loomed over the aisle, the jutting convolutions of the hulls like the promontories of a sandstone river canyon.

At last the salesman accompanied the couple to their Buick and saw them off with a hearty wave that looked like the casting of a spell to guarantee their return. He was a mountain of a man, muscular but lean—and handsome enough that Lisa took it as a challenge to pretend that she hadn't noticed. He wore a blue blazer, white trousers, and crepe-soled canvas shoes. The suntan beneath the bill of his yachting cap seemed the result of long hours on a boat deck.

He acknowledged Lisa with a nod and surreptitiously surveyed the parking lot to find her car and assess her financial status. "Well, see anything there you like?" He craned his neck to see if she had a male partner concealed in her hip pocket, then turned his attention to her with a glance that was sensual in its directness.

Suddenly aware of her tight jeans and high-heeled boots, she tugged self-consciously at her cropped black wig and nodded toward a nineteen-foot yellow-and-white semi-V. "How much is that one?"

Undecided whether to focus on business so soon, he silently gazed into her eyes, but presently his salesman's charm possessed him and he stepped aside to allow her to precede him up the metal steps.

"She's a beauty, all right. Take a look inside." His tone was sardonic, emphasizing that he was only going through the motions of a sale. Lisa remained on the ground, hands in pockets, knowing that he would be waiting to watch her thighs and bottom as she climbed the steep angle. Already his gaze had dropped.

"I've looked, it's very nice." She wondered what he would be like in bed. She had never been with so large a man and was tantalized by the prospect of his physical power. She imagined being lifted by his muscular arms, her legs wrapped around his trim waist. Looking up and gauging their relative heights, she realized that if he were inside her, his shoulders would clear the top of her head.

"Would you please tell me the price?" she asked.

"Price doesn't mean a thing unless you know what you're getting. Does your husband—"

"I'm alone." She stared at a tiny chip on his straight, white teeth. For a moment she forgot what they were discussing.

"Well now . . ." A smile of satisfaction as his gaze fell to her ring finger and he tried to discern whether alone meant available. He was too obvious, she decided. But he seemed so unconcerned about being forward that she kept watching herself to see if she was leading him on.

"I suppose you know how to handle a boat?" He was skeptical, assuming she would interpret his caution as concern.

"Please," she said. "Could you just tell me the price?"

"You're planning to take it out on the ocean?"

"Are your prices confidential perhaps?"

A slow smile curled his lips. Deciding to play it her way, he lazily opened a price list and quoted her the figures with exaggerated precision.

"Fine," she said. "But I'll need an alteration."

"What alteration?"

"A sort of locker cut into the flat part of the stern. It will open into the water from beneath the boat."

"*What?*" he scoffed, as bemused as if she had suggested that he make the cut with his teeth.

Originally she had planned to identify herself as a marine biologist who needed an underwater locker during rough weather for releasing gear directly into the ocean rather than over the side, like Cousteau's diving tube on the *Calypso*. But now she decided not to offer any explanation at all. She rather enjoyed provoking him.

"Perhaps I should have the sales manager write this one up?" She took satisfaction in his look of quick reassessment.

"It would take some time to make those changes. . . ."

"I don't have time."

He glanced at his watch, then into her eyes with almost frightened frankness. For a moment he probed her expression, trying to spare himself the embarrassment of asking his question by anticipating her answer.

She held his gaze, curiously monitoring herself, wondering what she would say if he managed to get it out.

"Do you . . . have an hour?" he asked.

There it was. Not so terrifying once it was out in the open. And suddenly his embarrassment made him seem human; she almost liked the guy.

"I'm sorry," she said.

Quickly he looked away. "Of course not. I'm a fool."

That set it for her; the quick apology, the collapse of the front as if it had been smashed by a cannonball.

"No, wait . . ." She touched his arm.

His eyes darted to her hand and he held his arm rigid as if not to dislodge her touch.

"I don't usually do this kind of thing . . ." she fumbled, disgusted by her triteness, then suddenly feeling bold. *What the hell,* she thought. There was a good chance she'd be dead in a month. Who was to care if she had this last pleasure?

He lived on a boat that was docked a five-minute walk from the sales lot. It was a two-masted wooden beauty he had renovated himself, a low-slung ketch lightly wavering in the ocean swells. Lisa was completely silent, and so was he, except to issue warnings about the slick deck and the narrow steps.

As they descended into the living quarters, he took her hand to guide her into the bedroom. Sitting on the double mattress which was snugly fitted into the bow, he stood her between his long thighs as if she were a toy soldier he was examining for chipped paint.

"Hey," he said softly, smiling at her stiffness. He put a hand on her cheek, and the fingers were long enough to reach around to the back of her neck. She closed her eyes and cocked her head, cradling his hand between her cheek and shoulder, then she felt herself being gently lifted as if she weighed no more than a puppy. Swinging free in the air, she swooned at the power of his arms and became light-headed as he laid her back on the pillows.

She opened her eyes to see him tugging off his blazer and shirt. His chest rippled with the movement of his muscles, which were smooth and long like a runner's. The shirt caught on his wrists because he had forgotten to undo the buttons, binding him like an extended pair of handcuffs. Sitting up, she ducked under the jacket and leaned back on the cloth so that the tension prevented his getting to the buttons. With a quiet smile in her eyes she pulled off her shirt and bra.

At the sight of her breasts he bent up his knees to trap her in the deep valley at his groin. He fumbled wildly to free his hands, finally ripping out a cuff, which hung loosely around his arm, tattered where it had torn from the shirt. With his free hand he pulled off the other button, then grasped her around the waist and lifted her in the air as he lay back on the bed to admire her pendulous breasts hanging free.

As his lips closed over one of her nipples and then the entire tip of her breast, her head dropped forward at the pleasure of it, and she reached out for his shoulders to steady herself against a sudden rocking of the boat. Sliding to his chest, she kissed his ears, forehead, and the palms of his hands as he lifted them from her body and began to unzip her jeans.

It occurred to her as she unbuckled his belt that even though she could never tell Phillip about her extraordinary effort in his behalf, she was doing him a considerable favor by ensuring that the boat alterations would be finished in time.

EIGHT

Slumped behind the wheel of a bureau Dodge, his chest aching from lack of sleep and his eyes stinging from the smog which pervaded the Westside with the cloying presence of aerosol hairspray, John sipped at his coffee for the caffeine alone, having lost any taste for the flavor five cups ago.

As he drove under the San Diego Freeway overpass, a boy in a jazzed up Camaro blasted a horn that played a dozen notes of the *Star Wars* theme. Irritably John imagined the car crashing off the road and collapsing at the base of a concrete stanchion into an electric-orange lump.

The evening session with Kaplan, followed by twelve grinding hours of suppressed hysteria while a bureau task force was assembled, had left him emotionally dead to everything except the need to carry through with routine, to approach this case like any other. This morning he had called Dr. Lewis at the RAM Corp think tank and set up a consultation, requesting information on likely bomb targets. To camouflage his real interest, he had mentioned freeway overpasses, power stations, and landmark structures, finally slipping in an offhanded reference to major dams.

When he had first discovered the brochures on Hoover Dam in Lisa's apartment, he had hoped that they were only tourist junk. But the margins had been full of notations on the security measures, number of guards, and positioning of boats and electric lights. In one of the photographs a flippant sketch of a smiling mushroom cloud had been penciled in above the highway which ran along the top of the dam.

Initially he had been relieved that Lisa's only apparent target was located in a sparsely populated Nevada desert. But after thinking about the consequences of an atomic explosion that would knock out Hoover Dam, and subsequently the villages and towns downstream, he had found it impossible to believe that Lisa was actually involved in such a monstrous scheme. Although he was fascinated by her nerve, his revulsion short-circuited his compassion. In retrospect he could pinpoint all sorts of craziness in her behavior—strange intensities in her eyes, hints of dementia in her voice, malicious double meanings in her words. But he knew he would immediately reverse his judgments if he suspected that she was an unwilling or ignorant participant—though the probability of that innocence seemed so low now as to be negligible.

During questioning by one of the more than two hundred agents brought onto the case, a Consolidated Atomic guard had identified Lisa from a photo that John had found at her apartment as the Western Union driver making a delivery the week of the uranium disappearance, possibly on the day a questionable suicide attempt had drawn workers to a rear fence in what now appeared to have been a diversionary tactic. But Western Union assured the bureau that Lisa had never been a bona fide employee and that none of their trucks were missing, so the recent registrations of the type of GMC van used in the delivery were being checked for leads.

The majority of other agents on the case were deployed at Hoover Dam. They remained under the direction of the Los Angeles office to sidestep the dubious security of the Vegas office, which had been called into question by disclosures of organized crime payoffs to Nevada agents. FBI sharpshooters equipped with telescopic rifles were posted every hundred feet along the crest of the canyon walls bordering the entrance to the dam, and they carried walkie-talkies for alerting other agents fishing on the river. Some of the men were trained in scuba and underwater recovery on the off-chance that something might be thrown over the wall of the highway before it could be diverted.

By this evening the Army Corps of Engineers would begin a report on the dam's ability to withstand nuclear blast. But given the caution of the Bureau of Reclamation since the Teuton Dam collapse their official conclusions would likely incubate awhile before being released. So the more immediate sources of information required priming.

Exiting from the freeway, John became mired in the lunch hour traffic from Santa Monica High School—fleets of motorcycles, ten-speed bicycles, and mural-sided vans. He watched a swirl of long blond hair distorted through a van's triangular porthole and pondered the deprivations of his youth when the cracked plastic seat of his dad's Volkswagen was the only alternative to an open field. Wistfully he contemplated blending with the crowd, swinging onto a stool of the corner pastrami stand where the specialty was inelegantly named *Double Meat* and whiling away the afternoon people-watching the students and freaks.

It was an old impulse, stronger for always being denied—an impulse to flee when things became too much for him. He thought of himself as supporting evidence for the theory that the intelligence services, like the armed forces, attracted not the most aggressive and adventurous of men, but the most peaceful. Those who were as disposed to sink into the bureaucratic muddle as into a warm bath, making not the slightest of waves. Surely all the other agents he knew were alike in that regard—law school graduates who disdained the risks of private practice and tolerated the boredom of the bureau for the compensating security and illusions of importance.

He negotiated a three-block gauntlet of bumper-to-bumper traffic and turned into the parking lot of the RAM Corp think tank, noting twin reflections from binoculars on the roof as evidence of new security procedures. Attempts at infiltration by foreign spies had always been relatively common—the tanks storing as many top secret government documents as CIA headquarters—but after Ellsberg had embarrassed RAND by sneaking out with a full briefcase, security had been stepped up at all the tanks.

The square, three-story building was surrounded by a chain link fence and looked as ordinary as a public high school—but the casualness was only a facade. The receptionist wore a .357 Magnum which creaked ominously in its leather holster as she logged him in and issued him a visitor's badge.

On the top floor he stepped from the elevator into a narrow gray hall which was lined with doors as closely spaced as the cells of a prison, each bearing a nameplate of the inmate within. The few men walking the row moved as gravely as guards, avoiding eye contact as if to avert the begging of favors.

Pausing at the window of a crisscrossing passageway, he watched some men in three-piece suits play an awkward game of Ping-Pong in an interior yard, clutching up their strokes to prevent welling-over sweat glands. John smiled at the similarity in atmosphere with bureau headquarters, RAM Corp having absorbed the flavor of the only client wealthy enough to afford its services: the U.S. Government.

A handwritten note taped above Dr. Lewis's office nameplate directed John to a steel door at the end of the hall. He opened it onto a dark stairway leading up to a room on the roof and felt a quickening of interest. Could this be the renowned "pit"?

He padded up and paused at the top, his head just clearing the stairwell, transfixed by the image projected on the round walls—a continuous, encircling panorama of a Rocky Mountain meadow. Creased by streams and backed by cloud-frosted mountain peaks, its fields were alive with weeds, wildflowers, and fallen trees. Birdcalls issued from concealed stereo speakers to a sonorous sound track of wheezing wind and hollowly bubbling water.

Complete with cushioned canvas floor and random throw pillows, the "pit" had been added in the late sixties, at the height of the revolt era, when the thinkers of the tanks were sensitive to charges of being sterile, uptight, and establishment-stale. RAM's answer was to provide a creative atmosphere for solving world problems. But as John heard it, the pit had become an oasis for after-lunch naps and romantic interludes, which had everyone enamored with it far beyond the original projections.

His eyes still attuned to the brightness of the projected image, he squinted out blindly over the canvas. At eye level with the floor, he was confident Lewis had not yet spotted him in the darkness, and he felt strangely cozy in the role of spy, like a mouse peering from its hole. With deliberate stealth he inched up on the stairs, and in the reflected blue light of a mountain peak he saw Lewis at the rim of the room, ensconced in a pen of pillows and looking so utterly despondent as to be a gaping hole draining all contentment from the Rockies idyll. His mouth was slack with despair, his eyes dead and—guilty?

Could this moroseness be a reaction to the phone call from the bureau he had made to Lewis earlier this morning, asking for estimates on the yields of bombs which could be fabricated from the missing Consolidated Atomic uranium? He had tried to cloak his request in great, billowing clouds of abstractness and indifference, seeming only to want to be prepared in the unlikely instance that Lewis's convictions on the uranium disappearance proved valid. But it seemed apparent that Lewis had seen through the charade and felt personally anguished by the bureau's implied confirmation of the theft. Could the man possibly think his campus lectures bore major responsibility for inciting some nut to action? It seemed absurd. . . .

Embarrassed by his spying, John silently retreated down the stairs, then noisily opened and closed the door and trudged up with a heavier tread.

Turning up the overhead light at a console on the wall, Lewis was leaning against the pillows with a self-possession so natural that John questioned whether the distress of moments before hadn't been a trick of the shadows. Could any man so readily compose himself from dejection to casual good humor?

The greeting never making it to his eyes, Lewis smiled by tucking in the corners of his mouth. "I was feeling lazy today. Thought you'd enjoy seeing the pit. But if you'd rather go back to my office . . ."

"No, it's fine. I like it." John kicked off his shoes and traversed the padding to sit against a pillow propped up on the wall.

Sitting Indian fashion on the floor, Lewis gazed at a writing pad in his lap. "So I was right. . . ."

"About what?" asked John, but Lewis's look proscribed any evasion, and finally John shrugged. "The bureau simply wants to be prepared."

"Sure." Lewis pushed over a Manila folder, which—astonishingly—contained a report on Hoover Dam's vulnerability to nuclear blast.

John looked it over and tried to decide what to make of it. Reviewing the morning's telephone conversation with Lewis, he realized his attempts to obscure his interest in dams had been transparent. But even so Lewis had made a damned good guess. He felt Lewis watching with a hint of self-satisfied challenge, somewhat relishing the discomfort he had provoked. But behind the eyes lurked a trace of veiled fear—perhaps a nervousness that he had gone too far, set too much in motion.

Lewis seemed to read his thoughts and looked pleased at having struck home. "I thought like a terrorist to figure that one. Grand Coulee is much more massive, but Hoover holds back nearly twice the water—more power for devastation with less resistance. And then there's the symbolic element, which Hoover wins hands down. RAM Corp has prepared lots of those reports on domestic war targets for the Defense Department, so I just plucked that one from the files."

Choosing not to pay the expected compliment on the man's canny deduction, John remained with the point at hand. "Where would someone try to hit it?"

"I assume they'd drop a bomb into the reservoir behind the dam where it's most vulnerable to lateral thrust."

"By air?"

"Not unless they're stupid and suicidal. They'd need an accurate hit, and getting down low enough would put them right in the blast."

So, Lewis had it all figured out—and perhaps had missed his real calling as a federal investigator. Certainly he looked as much like an agent as a physicist. John expected scientists to be slightly homely, physically unsuited for the more social occupations—not strikingly handsome with the high level of animal tension that Lewis seemed to radiate.

John closed the file. "Is there some way a dam could be protected?"

"Nope, afraid not. Shouldn't be built in the first place. A series of lower, thinner dams would require less concrete and steel. And gravity-fed irrigation is dying out anyway; so there's no reason to build dams that are strategically rewarding targets. You hit one of them and wipe out most of the towns downstream, along with all the water and hydroelectric for a huge area."

So this is how he's going to work it, thought John. Even though Lewis clearly understood that the threat was real and immediate, he was mocking the bureau's speculations with broad theories of his own as if the only objectives of the consultation were safer standards for future dams. But John decided to take the instruction as it fell. "Doesn't the engineering for the larger dams make them less vulnerable to a blast?"

"At the base. But who says a dam had to be blown at the base? Hoover is a wedge tapering at the top. A lot of its depth is for silt storage, because Colorado River water is a kind of thin mud, so a hole well above the bottom could still empty Lake Mead."

"And with a hundred and fifty miles of water I suppose the pressure would be tremendous?"

"If pressure depended on mass, you'd blow out your eardrums swimming in the ocean."

"Well, then the power, or whatever, of that volume of water."

"Yes, it would be something." Lewis sounded almost

wistful, but apparently realized the indecorousness of his affection for disaster and came as close to looking embarrassed as John had ever seen him. "Of course, it's improbable that amateurs could generate enough energy to blast the dam all the way through. Even a decent atomic bomb won't blow up everything; a lot depends on placement."

"Would it have to be positioned right on the concrete?"

"Should be close; the shock wave would travel over a certain distance, but they'd lose a lot of the fireball to steam if they were too far away. A line of buoys about three hundred yards upriver keeps the boats away from the rear of the dam, so I'd guess that the highway over the top is where they're likely to drop it."

Nodding blank-faced, John was amused at Lewis's presumption in thinking that his elementary speculation could be instructive. The FBI had a dozen experts poring over diagrams of the dam, deciding upon points of physical vulnerability and methods of sealing them off. A cable strung across the river entrance, entirely blocking the water access, had been considered but ultimately rejected because the river canyon formed as nice a trap as could be devised. And catching Lisa and her tribe was preferred to scaring them off with obtrusive security measures.

Lewis pushed over the pad covered with his calculations. "Those are some reasonable limits on the yield of a bomb. I can't tell you anything with certainty, because we don't really understand underwater bursts or the plastic state of structural materials stressed beyond the elastic limit—particularly under dynamic loads. But offhand I'd say that at those lower values the dam wouldn't suffer significant damage. At the upper limits who can say? But I wouldn't be shocked if the whole thing went. The Teuton Dam was only half full when it collapsed, and still it generated a fifty-foot wall of water that knocked out entire cities. Add the effects of radiation, with a full reservoir many times the size, and you've got a mammoth calamity. The fallout would be lethal within a mile radius, and you'd have a raging flood of radioactive water for hundreds of miles."

"How do you visualize the sequence?" Was the question too committal? He tried to cover with the silly game of looking bored.

"First chunks of concrete as big as houses exploding out horizontally, crashing down on the people at the pumping works, then a wave of water maybe three hundred feet high raging down toward the lower dams, spilling over to flood the cities along the banks, all the way down into the Imperial Valley and Mexico."

"The lower dams couldn't stop it?"

Lewis smiled as if at a backward student. "Parker and Davis dams are kept nearly full. Any extra water would go over them like a ball rolling down a flight of stairs. Hoover retains enough water to flood the state of Connecticut to a depth of ten feet; that's five thousand gallons for every person on earth. Nothing could hold it back. You'd get damage in the billions and deaths in the thousands."

He leaned over and started punching buttons on the

console, no more ruffled than if he had delivered a lecture on Maxwell's equations. The scene on the walls abruptly flashed to a Pacific seashore at sunset, and the stereo tapes to crashing waves and screeching gulls. After allowing a moment for John's appreciation he changed the scene to Central Park with the Manhattan skyline above the trees in the distance and the stereo sounds of muted traffic, barking dogs, and laughing children.

"For transferred Easterners," explained Lewis.

John dug into his pocket for a copy of the photograph he had taken from Lisa's apartment. The cropped enlargement showed only her face. He wanted to get out of here; the static travelogue was beginning to wear. "Do you recognize this woman from any of your lectures? Light-brown hair, blue eyes. About twenty-eight?"

As if pleased to be finally taking part in something that was recognizable as FBI business—*Identifying the Suspect*—Lewis studied the photo with interest, and for a moment John could have sworn he read recognition on his face. But Lewis shook his head decisively. "I could say yes, I guess. She's got one of those faces—all-American, very familiar. You see them on television in ads. To me they all look alike. But no—not specifically this girl. I don't remember her."

"Oh, well . . ." said John, unaccountably relieved. He glanced at the table and tore off the page of calculations, then gaped at the drawing beneath, a labeled sketch of a homemade uranium bomb. "That gun barrel. Would a bazooka be about the right size?"

"Oh, sure. Just about perfect." Lewis started to go into all the nuances of construction for the perfect job, but John's mind would not focus; it resonated with the sounds of honking taxis on Fifth Avenue and horses' hooves clopping on the pavement in Central Park in hollow, deathly thuds.

NINE

Phillip counted his heartbeats for ten seconds and multiplied by six for a pulse of a hundred and eight—eighteen higher than an hour before, a respectable gain. He remembered having heard that chronic risk-takers were addicted to their own secretions of adrenaline and calculated that tomorrow's excitement would put him higher over the moon than the best heroin on the street.

The uranium slug felt silky between his palms, and he lingered in his appreciation. For a moment he even considered signing his name along its length—as GI's were said to have initialed the bullets they used on Nazis—but declined that bit of glory as sentimental foolishness.

Tipped by an initiator and tamper cap, the slug was screwed to a modified bazooka shell, wired to an alarm-clock detonator. The clock was regrettable but necessary because a radio signal would not penetrate the river's depths. The bomb lay at his feet, encased in a watertight six-foot plastic drainage pipe, sealed at one end by an eyelet cap. Along the top were strapped a lead weight diving belt, an underwater propulsion unit, a length of nylon rope, and four diving vests fed by a tank of compressed air through a manifold valve.

Carefully loading the shell into the breech, he felt a sense of peace and thought how far he had come in learning to handle his lifelong obsessions. Finally he was listening to his blood.

The phrase popped to mind: *listening to his blood*. How eerie it sounded now, oozing out of the past as it had, coming loose from some capillary in his brain like a clot to produce a stroke. The phrase had haunted him all through childhood, the bane of his early life. But somehow he hadn't thought of it in years. The first time he had heard it was . . . when? Almost thirty years ago. . . .

Father's Day, second grade—the worst day of all. It settled upon him with the weight of a bull, pinning him flat in the mud, gasping for breath, with no chance of ever working free. He was dressed by a maid in a tight little sailor's suit and taken from his mother's apartment to his father's house. On the way he was coached on respectful silence, the art of melting into the walls and avoiding his father's ire. For reasons he had never understood, his relationship with his father was a miasma of despair. He didn't try to figure it out, sensing the inkling of an answer in his own slimy self, avoiding a guilt that would be too painful to face. He knew it had something to do with his parents' separation, which had occurred shortly after his birth, but any further curiosity represented a danger he couldn't risk. Something about him was

fundamentally wrong. Why else would his father refuse to speak to him, to meet his eyes, to eat or play
with him?

His mother seemed to think that the clay ashtray he
had made in school held the beginnings of a solution.
Something so simple! Why hadn't they thought of it
before? He had never given his father a gift! Something to heal the wounds and break the silence. Per-
suaded by her confidence, he dared to hope for
acceptance.

As the butler showed them into his father's den, his
mother seemed to shrink. Acting coyly antic although
her face was lined with age, she made a fool of herself
trying to please, as if begging forgiveness for some un-
mentionable sin. His father treated her girlishness
with scorn, and she nudged Phillip forward, as if to
handle problems she found unmanageable.

Finding it hard to see straight, Phillip clutched the
gift so tightly the wrapping puckered with perspiration as he jerked himself over to the desk and deposited his present on the edge.

For a moment, he felt the room tilt around him as
he waited for the judgment. Then unable to bear the
tension, he lifted his gaze to the wall's enormous ren-
dering of Hoover Dam and felt somewhat reassured.
He knew it intimately, having been raised on the ro-
mance of its construction: stories of his grandfather's
contributions as a civil engineer, his father's draftings
as a young college graduate, his mother's ministrations
as a site nurse. In Boulder City his parents had met
and married; her wedding bouquet had been en-

tombed within the concrete as a gesture of eternal fidelity. . . .

Assessing the package on the desk, his father fingered the crude handwritten card with its filial sentiment copied from the blackboard, his eyes narrowed with disgust and dismay. Without undoing the wrapping, he shoved the present back at his wife, the action a reproach to her presumption and an insistence on old patterns.

Her face lost its coquettish softness and took on a hardness that seemed to have been lurking beneath the surface, ready to rise if necessary. She started to whine, and her vitriol broke the resolve of seven years silence. Phillip crawled under an end table and tried to become deaf. He looked up at Hoover Dam and suddenly felt shamed by its greatness. As much as he resented his father's aloofness, the dam seemed to symbolize an ability that Phillip felt he could never match.

In time he knew his parents assumed that he had fled the room. His mother spoke of "the child" and searched around the furniture, then flew at his father with private fierceness.

His father flung the package into the trash. His voice was deep and furious. "My son is dead! His murderer's bastard won't replace him!"

The words crackled in Phillip's brain like an electric current aligning the mysteries that had always plagued him. As he listened with numb curiosity, his parent's innuendos fell into a hazy pattern which he only fully understood with the passage of time.

One moonless night eight years before, a man with a

nylon stocking over his head broke into the house and made his way up to the master bedroom to pilfer cash and jewels. As an afterthought, a final defilement, he had raped Phillip's mother while his bound-and-gagged father looked on, then he tied her up and forced her to witness the sodomizing of her husband. When their eighteen-year-old son heard noises and came to investigate, the man executed him with a bullet through the neck. Three months later his forty-two-year-old mother discovered she was pregnant, and in her grief for the slain child refused to abort the fetus, even though it was known not to be her husband's. . . .

While Phillip cowered under the end table, his parents shouted in unison, their accusations ramming head-on for mutual destruction. Compulsively they probed—and wounded, obsessed in spite of their apparent affection. Making it clear that Phillip could never be more than a reminder of a night of horror that had cost him his integrity, his wife, and his beloved heir, his father vowed that if it were up to him alone, the "bastard would be back on the streets in the old man's business of thieving for a living." If his wife wanted more money than he was providing, she could turn her bastard loose on the neighborhood—"He's got all the vile instincts to get anything he wants if he'll just listen to his blood."

With a schoolboy's vengeance Phillip looked out from under the table at the dam's great rising wall of concrete, which seemed so unyielding, granting nothing in its effortless restraint of ten trillion gallons of water. And he swooned at the thought of blowing the thing apart, imagining its spectacular demolition, the awesome mounds of rubble that would rise from the riverbed once the mountainous wave rolled free.

Consumed with the fantasy, he failed to notice that he had leaned out far enough to be visible. His reward for the carelessness was seeing his father blanch with shame.

All the way home his mother sobbed against Phillip's neck. Holding him in her lap and cradling his hands, she kept calling him her "poor, poor boy," assuring him that she would always take care of him. But she was too mortified to look him in the face, which explained his expulsion from the nest to a military academy the following week.

A Christmas card informed him of his parents' reunion, and it was his last direct contact with either of them. Every holiday, visiting day, school play, vacation, and graduation, he awaited their appearance, until a fellow student, who had also been forgotten over an Easter vacation, taught him the thrill of standing up to rejection. Using a Tampax dipped in wax as a fuse, they exploded a can of gunpowder emptied from rifle shells at one of his father's construction sites, burning the timbers to ashes before the fire department arrived.

Retaliation was a wonderful sedative. Phillip began to feel a little better. After the blast he discovered fresh rewards in his science classes and learned to find the means of his relief in the school library. On visiting days, while watching the other children frolic with their parents, he coolly calculated how to maximize his fun over the upcoming holiday. All during the fall he would collect supplies for Christmas: pipes, wires, fuses, batteries, terminals, and gunpowder.

When the last of his schoolmates had left to visit their families, he would retreat to his room, construct a device, and ride a bus downtown. He always went on a Sunday, when fewer people were around, to capitalize on the low-risk factor. His favorite tactic was to find a deserted store that had a large mail drop slot in the seedy section of Olvera Street. He used traps baited with peanut butter as his triggering devices to add the suspense of having rats set the things off.

After the blast, when the fire trucks barreled in to put out the blaze, he would mingle with the crowd and exchange speculations, glorying in his facade of innocence while inwardly laughing at his deception.

Eventually, as his devices grew in complexity, he learned that a sufficiently difficult target could produce moments of transcendence. When he finally decided on Hoover Dam as his crowning achievement, the challenge alone was more fulfilling than all his previous successes.

Of course, he had had to fight with Lisa about accepting it as a serious target. Never having known his parents, she couldn't appreciate the perfect irony of a cowering little boy's fantasies under an end table becoming a triumphant reality. Instead she had been fixated on hallowed landmarks like the Empire State Building, the Capitol, or the Statue of Liberty—with a wry suggestion of deepening the Grand Canyon to make it even grander.

But in his own mind there had never been any doubt about the eventual target. He thought it pointless to bring down anything that some jerk with a sufficient load of TNT could level. His target was to be invincible, majestic, and unassailable. It was to be his family's dam, no question about it. . . .

Outside a car screeched to a halt, and the inside garage door crashed against the wall.

Flushing and scowling, Lisa strode inside with her fists jammed in the pockets of her leather jacket. "Did you hear the news?"

"Hear what?" He reached for the milk on the workbench, his stomach burning with acid, which was more worrisome to him as a sign of doubt than as a symptom of ulcers.

"A bunch of nuts on the Hollywood Freeway just tried to steal an ICBM tipped with a nuclear warhead."

Feeling cheated somehow, he sank to the stool, dismayed that strangers shared so intimate a vision and goal. "Did they get it?"

"No, the driver got away, thank God. It was coming from Tennessee to Long Beach, and four guys in a car tried to force it over to the shoulder, but the truck driver radioed the cops."

"So we're okay."

Less philosophical, Lisa stabbed a T square into a block of pattern wax. "What a bunch of jerk-offs! Couldn't even steal the finished product, when we started from scratch!"

Catching her eye, he tried to elicit a smile. Being forced to live together the last few days was making both of them irritable. Lisa was afraid to return to her apartment for fear that it would be staked out by the

FBI, and the deprivation of solitude was pushing her toward the edge. In the past, whenever they had had their fill of togetherness they would withdraw to their own homes, keeping a buffer zone of several miles between them. Now the biggest separation they could manage was the hundred feet between the laboratory and the house.

"You ready?" he asked.

In answer she jangled a ring of keys and pressed a button to lift the garage door. The boat stood in the driveway, mounted on a special trailer that was adapted to provide access to the trap door in the hull. A row of plastic cushions over the protrusion in the boat's interior gave the appearance of additional seating area. Lisa climbed into the attached van and backed up a few inches at a time while he sighted along the pipe to guide the boat directly over it.

Using the auto jacks in tandem, they pumped the bomb into the boat's chamber, securing it in place with steel cable slings bolted inside.

He lowered the jacks and slammed the trap door. "Everything packed?"

"Yep. Just have to water the plants."

TEN

The map of Nevada was strictly for tourists. It was cutely illustrated, with tennis and swimming opportunities pinpointed by courts and diving boards that appeared to mark off several square miles in area. Distances were foreshortened or exaggerated as suited the artist's aesthetics, and the roads labeled only when the letters could be squeezed between sketches of fish, boats, airplanes, shopping bags, beer steins, and smiling suns.

Although Phillip knew that by now he had to be within twenty miles of the dam—a major American landmark—he had yet to spot a single goddamn sign indicating its location, and he vowed that in the future he would confine his activities to California, where the highways were perfect and the point-of-interest signs ubiquitous.

He hunched down in the passenger seat of the van and shoved the map to the floor, disgruntled that the route from Henderson to Boulder City was represented by an unmarked thread. Lisa had driven the route a few months earlier but claimed not to remember the highway number, though he suspected she was being vague only to rile him. Ever since they had passed through Vegas, where the temperature had lingered in the high nineties, the tension had been running between them like static electricity on a dry day.

"We need gas," he said.

"I have eyes." She drove right past a Standard station to belie his control, and when she finally pulled into a Mobil, she snatched up her overnight bag and marched straight to the washroom, leaving him to instruct the elderly attendant on duty. His stomach knotting like a fist over a handful of nails, he directed the old man to fill the tank and then walked back to a grocery store to buy a quart of milk which he gulped from the carton.

Lisa was still in the washroom when he returned, so he slid into the driver's seat, grateful at least that he would no longer have to abide her stubbornness at the wheel.

Wistfully the old man examined the boat while counting out Phillip's change. "Always liked a yellow boat. Wanted one like it my whole life. Had her long?"

"A year or so." Phillip unfolded the map and had the man identify the route, his cracked and oily finger leaving gray smudges over the smiling sun like obscuring clouds of doom.

"What do you fish for?" asked the man.

"Oh, nothing special." Phillip looked at the billboard over the grocery store, which read: "TROJANS! They LAST longer!" The attendant drifted off to take care of another customer, keeping his eyes on the windshield of a Fiat, not deigning to acknowledge Lisa's striking appearance as she emerged from the washroom looking like a hip Mexican whore. Her skin was stained with bronzer; her eyes were ringed with heavy mascara; her lips were rouged with purplish lipstick. Over her forehead down to her blackened eyebrows she had pulled a black wig and a gypsy cap-scarf, but her most flagrant transformations were the ballooning breasts and padded hips beneath a Disneyland T-shirt and Frederick's of Hollywood Capri slacks.

She slid into the passenger seat, and Phillip pulled back into traffic, silenced by her disguise, which was as effective as mirrored sunglasses in discouraging eye contact. But as they entered the residential outskirts of a small town, she turned to him with challenge in her voice.

"You're going to the dam first, aren't you?"

He shook his head from side to side, knowing that if the dam were to be his prey, he would have to approach it as a hunter striking suddenly upon coming out of the gloom, shooting from the hip without the intimidation of prior encounter. But Lisa could never appreciate the more subtle aspects of the stalk because she had not participated in the selection of the quarry.

"You'll have to go alone," he said. "After we unload the gear at the lake, you can make sure everything's normal at the dam."

He tried not to see the kids spinning back on their banana-seat bicycles in the Dairy Queen parking lot or the ten-foot-square sign reading: "SMILE! YOU'RE

IN BOULDER CITY." The mundaneness of local life intruded on the drama of his mission.

Just beyond the Lake Mead Tourist Center, he turned to the Hemmenway boat launch, an effete patch of earth bordering the lake which was striking in its barren desolation and muddy uniformity. A dozen Airstream trailers were clustered at its center like a handful of silver jelly beans on an earthenware platter. Ringed by motorcycles and portable barbecues, mute players sat in dour groups of four at foldup cardtables, sipping beer and looking dazed by the combinations in their hands.

"No dry run," ho said. "I'll set the clock and seal the pipe as soon as you get back."

"You're sure you don't want to come with me to check out the dam?" Her tone was mothering and chiding, as if cautioning him against any impetuosity he might regret.

With a finality that made her blanch beneath her bronzer his eyes went glass-hard, and he swung the van around and backed the boat up to the floating dock, which was mounted on pontoons to accommodate the fluctuations in the lake's shoreline as the level of the dam rose and fell. It occurred to him that tonight the dock would have to be moved several miles out if it were still to float in the waters of the Colorado.

The surrounding hills were tinged with a reddish, otherworldly cast like great piles of modeling clay, totally devoid of vegetation. At the highway's crest Lisa shifted the van into second for the descent to the dam, feeling a giddy fear at the scope of what they had taken upon themselves. The craggy mountain peaks of the once unflooded land rose like islands from the gray waters of Lake Mead, their majesty shrouded by the dammed-up river flow which seemed a glimmering desert mirage.

She wanted to stop and take it all in with stern doses of reassurance, but she forced herself to continue on to the souvenir stand's parking lot which was bordered by the stone wall of the river canyon, its profile turreted like a medieval castle. A troop of girl scouts leaned out over the wall, vying for close-up photos and propping one another up in the foreground to claim for themselves some reflection of Hoover's grandeur.

With eyes carefully averted Lisa moved to a deserted stretch, pressed her knees against the cool stone, and straightened her wig to keep it from slipping back beneath the loose scarf. Quickly she lifted her gaze.

Even though daily she had imagined the vastness of her target, seeing it again stirred in her a sense of shock at her own audacity. The dam's arched face was a cresting, concrete tidal wave and seemed to challenge her to visualize the cinematics of its break, the very instant of its bursting. Perhaps at first a hairline crack in the bowl, then all would give way at once. . . .

Beyond the souvenir stand a woman with a pronounced Brooklyn accent screamed at her teen-aged son not to touch the wall, as if her experience with structural restraints were limited to pastry shells. Lisa eyed her with heavy disgust, then turned her attention to a group of tourists marching in submissive rows on the pumping works at the dam's base, sublimely ignorant of their impending fate—to be washed away like a column of ants under the force of a garden hose. Regrettably it would all go unrecorded on film, although as a media event the destruction would surely rank with the explosion of the Hindenburg and the Alaskan earthquake.

Taking a camera from the van, she strolled onto the dam itself and crossed to the upriver side of the highway, looking through the telephoto lens at the coast guard cutter which bobbed at the reservoir's dock with the passivity of a dreaming guard, habitually untended and never untethered. A few men fished in rented outboards beyond the buoys or gawked back at her through their own telephotos, and she lowered the camera to regard the pale water that lapped at the intake towers inside the buoy line. She puzzled for a moment over the position of the line. It seemed to be farther away than the three hundred yards Phillip had estimated, but she dismissed the concern with a reminder that she had never been a judge of distances exceeding fifteen feet.

Her focus was drawn to a queue of people waiting for a tour into the dam's interior. A fat man at the head of the line was struggling to wrench a bite from a chocolate taffy bar, his neck muscles taut and cordy with strain, his face distorted into a growl, until a guide abruptly singled him out with a sharp reprimand against eating on tour. Sheepishly the man ducked his head and whisked the wrapper over the tooth-dented candy, penitently jamming it into his pocket as the group scurried toward a waiting elevator and jockeyed for positions of alliance with the guide.

Swinging the camera at her side, Lisa strode back to the van, thinking it unfortunate that so obsequious a bunch could get mileage from the claim that they had been among the last to make the tour—unless of course they dallied too long today, in which case they would be taking a final dip in Lake Mead during its disappearance.

ELEVEN

The housing tract in Westchester was less than a mile from Los Angeles International Airport, and the periodic rumble of passing jets set the beat of life for the staunchly middle-class neighborhood. At dusk the lights flicking on in the rows of homes threatened to drown the grayish glow of television screens shining through the drapes. From several sets at once sounded the opening refrain of a local news program, followed by the rhythmic pulsing that portended events of consequence.

Climbing from his car, John attempted to sidestep the investigation of a ragged mutt, but resigned himself to sending his suit to the cleaners when the animal's filthy coat made an odorous sweep against his pants legs. For a moment he considered going back to the office. This interview would probably turn out to be a waste of time. Gathering firsthand testimony about the progression of underwater atomic explosions seemed lame at this point, but he had no leads of any promise and felt compelled to keep moving, however futile his efforts proved to be.

A teen-aged boy watched him from the porch, then

glared from under surly brows and cut across the lawn as if to avoid sharing the sidewalk.

John tried a smile. "Is your dad around?"

The boy cocked his head toward the garage, his eyes remaining black with suspicion, and John recognized himself ten years earlier and wondered at the boy's aloofness to a fellow traveler. But rapprochement seemed impossible. Wordlessly he passed through the gate to the little courtyard at the front of the house, shutting out the whining dog on the lawn and continuing through the open side door of the garage.

Inside a man with a full head of white hair brushed rudely back was dissecting the innards of a machine on the floor. His face was tanned and rutted with cynicism, and his stern visage seemed in keeping with the seriousness of his telephone voice, which had been pitched unnaturally low, as if striving for something of worth in the depths.

"I appreciate your seeing me on such short notice," said John. "Dr. Lewis assured me that Sam Hibbert was the man to see about the underwater blasts at Bikini Beach."

"You know, you're the first person in ten years who didn't think that meant I'd surfed with Annette Funicello in a beach movie." He grinned at the joke, which seemed a standard rejoinder, and John was struck by Hibbert's affability, which came close to docility and seemed so in contrast with his appearance.

Taking a seat above the dismantled machine, he watched Hibbert return to his work, apparently unconcerned that the bureau took an interest in his Bikini experiences, as he picked up a can of WD-40 and sprayed a mechanism.

"How long were you in the navy?" asked John.

"Army. Thirty-five years. Bikini was a joint task force of army, navy, and civilian personnel." He closed his teeth over his lips as if self-conscious about a new pair of dentures, then applied the full weight of his body on a screwdriver that was wedged into a mechanical linkage, producing a familiar series of whirrings and clinking gears.

"That isn't a slot machine—" asked John.

"Sure is; you've got a good ear. I took the reels off to replace the strips. You interested in coin machines?"

Hibbert waited for the nod, then waded through the tools and metal parts carpeting the floor to pull a plastic garbage bag from a chromed slot machine, its casing brilliantly gaudy with red, green, and yellow scroll insets surrounding a cast Indian head. The very crassness of the machine appealed to John and seemed to give it a strange authority, an aura of self-assured rebellion against imposed tastes and overly refined standards.

"Restoring is my hobby," said Hibbert. "I needed something to keep me busy after I retired, and when the price of antique slots skyrocketed after they became legal, I was able to make a few bucks too. Wanna play it?"

"Sure."

"But with my money." His eyes wrinkled with amused cunning, as if he had just eluded an FBI vice trap for gambling. Dutifully he hunted out a coffee can full of dimes, and John plowed in a few coins, enjoying the raucous slappings of the mechanisms that were somehow more pleasing than the silent electronics of the modern machines. A cherry snapped into place on the first reel, clinking a few coins into the payout dish, and he dropped them back into the can.

"So Bikini used civilian personnel, too?"

"Oh, sure," said Hibbert. "We had marine biologists, oceanographers, photographers, chemists, journalists, doctors—well over forty thousand in all."

"And the only purpose was to test how our ships would stand up to an underwater explosion?"

"That and making the first underwater test of the bomb itself. We had everything out there that would float—German, Japanese, and American. Submarines, battleships, cruisers, seaplanes, destroyers . . . Even some concrete dry docks, I think."

"It must have been terrifying."

"Hell, yes. No one knew what to expect. Some of the experts were predicting a tidal wave that would wipe out the South Pacific islands, or a fissure in the ocean floor that would go clear to the molten center of the earth, or an unending nuclear chain reaction that would turn the planet into a dead star."

"And yet no one was harmed?"

"Not by the blast. But one of the ships was loaded down with animals to test the radioactivity—goats, pigs, rats. . . . I think maybe even some chickens and dogs. And most of them died."

"The bomb was anchored underwater?"

"It was suspended from a ship in a watertight, steel caisson and fired with a radio signal."

"Not a time fuse?"

"No way. When you've got that many people to evacuate, the firing had to be under control. Too much chance of a foul-up with a timed fuse."

Apparently bored with his story, Hibbert picked up a paper strip that was printed with bells and fruit and fed it under the staying ridges of a reel, his fingers moving surely in repetition of a familiar task. He fitted the reels to the machine, spun them lightly, and slid the mechanism into an aluminum casing, locking on its steel back.

"Let me show you something I found," he said. "Ought to interest an FBI man." Unfastening the back of a smaller machine, he rotated the reels to slip off a square of cardboard bearing a decal. "See these little ridges holding this lemon over the cherry? Whenever the casino wanted to pump up the odds in favor of the house, they'd cover one of the cherries on the first reel, then screw a cover over the readout hole to fool the machine into making fewer payoffs."

John examined the proffered evidence, but he was annoyed at being sidetracked and annoyed, too, at being forced to suppress every sense of urgency and alarm. "How long have you been collecting slots?"

"Oh, let me think." Hibbert grinned. "It's been legal for what—two years? So I guess I've only been collecting that long."

John smiled and returned to his perch on the stool, turning his back on the machines with the hope of dislodging Hibbert's focus. "Do you happen to remember how close the nearest target ship was to the bomb?"

"Well over five hundred feet, I'd say. An enormous battleship moored broadside. The *Arkansas*. I remember, because I won a bet on how she'd fare."

"She survived?"

"Nope, crumpled like a stepped-on Christmas bulb and sank instantly. Of course, the blast was putting more than twenty million tons of underwater pressure on her hull."

"What about harbor installations? Any docks, bridges, or dams?"

"Just the coral reefs, but they're strong as concrete, and the blast blew the hell out of them and took a couple million cubic yards of dirt out of the bottom of the lagoon. So any bridge or dam would have lost its footings for sure. They say the shock wave was the worst ever produced on earth."

"How long did it last?"

"A split second; it travels at the speed of sound, but there are secondary bubble pulses that increase the damage of the first big punch."

"Were you able to watch the actual explosion?"

"Yeah, through binoculars on a ship about fifteen miles away. But if you're looking for a factual description, I can't give it to you. I'm sure you'd get forty thousand different ones from the task force. Something like that is so far from normal experience that the brain just grabs for what sounds best, and no two people agree."

"I'd like to hear whatever you remember."

Hibbert gave a rueful sigh. "Well, first there was a blinding red flash. And then a roar that made me think I'd never used my ears before. The water glowed like searchlights were floating forty feet under. And up shot a column of water that was higher than five Empire State Buildings stacked tip to tip. It was half a mile in diameter and flattened into a mushroom cloud with the force of an earthquake. The tidal wave was a hundred feet high with whole battleships dropping off its sides as it plunged back into the lagoon. Then a thousand-foot surge of mist stormed out over the ocean at fifty miles an hour, like radioactive thunderheads—a rolling fogbank that killed the animals like rifleshots to their brains."

John had taken out a pad to make notes in his crude shorthand, but when he reached the bottom of a page, he stopped and his shoulders sagged. The magnitude of the possible disaster was beginning to lose impact for him in being so excessive.

"What about the ship suspending the bomb?" he asked.

"It disintegrated. Went up just like cigarette smoke." Hibbert fed some nickels into one of the machines, seemingly oblivious to the gaming aspects of gambling as he tested the slot's mechanical functioning. But apparently he was pleased with the few coins rattling into the payout dish.

"See that?" he asked. "Three plums and I only got twelve coins. These machines are designed for Liberty nickels which were thinner than the Buffalos, so now it shorts one or two."

He glanced over and saw that John had returned to his notes. "Guess this all seems crazy. You want to talk about the nuclear crisis and the world going to hell, and all I care about is fixing up old slot machines."

He smiled sardonically, but his eyes were bright, even proud. "You know, I wasted half my life getting mad about things I couldn't change, but after I retired, I realized I didn't give a good damn what happened as long as everything just held together until I died. Never did care probably. Just afraid to look so damn selfish."

Slowly, John folded up the pad and stuck it back in his pocket.

"Oh, you don't have to leave," said Hibbert. "I may not give a damn, but I kind of like talking it over with someone who does."

TWELVE

As the engine noise subsided and the screen of bubbles lifted, Phillip uncurled his hands from the steel bar bolted to the bottom of the boat and discovered to his relief that he had survived his underwater rampage down the river canyon with no more damage to himself than a raw upper gum from the current's pressure on his regulator mouthpiece.

Lulled by the sudden stillness, he lay in a deadman's float beneath the boat, the waters of Lake Mead fading from a putrid muck in the depths to a sunlit sparkle at the surface above, like a bottle of broth left long enough on the shelf to have separated into component layers.

Abruptly a pop-eyed fish swam out of the haze, then halted at a distance to scrutinize the intruder.

Phillip lifted an arm and exploded a fist in a five-fingered burst that made the fish disappear as if yanked from the water by a hook through its lip. Behind the tempered glass of his facemask his eyes squinted in delight. God, but he felt fine. All the doubts and hesitations of the day dissolved in the solitude of the lake where the only sound was the reassuring wheezing of his own breathing and where everything reduced to a matter of steady, automatic rhythm—inhale, kick, exhale, stroke. Nothing to think about, nothing to question.

A splash ended the quiet, and on the surface beside the boat wobbled a red-and-white fishing bobber, which he lowered by the lead sinker. He checked it for the compass heading to the center of the dam's face, but found written in bold grease pencil the substitute message—

No Go!

Fighting down a fury over Lisa's skittishness at the zero hour, he rubbed out the first word of the message with the tip of a gloved finger and sent the bobber leaping clear of the surface in a defiant pop. He would just have to guess at the compass heading, he decided as he yanked open the boat's underwater chamber door.

Sealed within the watertight plastic pipe, the bomb was in good shape, wearing several diver's buoyancy-compensator vests strapped around its girth. Through rubber tubing leading from a branched valve the vests were fed by a tank of compressed air, permitting adjustments for positive, negative, and neutral buoyancy that would cause the bomb to rise, sink, or remain at rest.

Pressing the flat spring-action inflation lever on the valve, Phillip released gas into the vests until the bomb was neutrally buoyant, then he unfastened its chamber latches and allowed it to move from its berth as gently as an infant whale swimming from the womb. It was attached by a nylon umbilical cord to a free-floating bullet-shaped diver's watercycle.

With his fins grazing the boat's hull he grasped the handles of the cycle, switched on its motor, and lurched abruptly downward as the cycle took up slack in the rope, then slowed in accepting the weight of the bomb. As he passed beyond the boat's protective canopy, his descent steepened acutely, and a stream of water seeped through the neck of his wet suit, displacing the body-warmed layer and making him shiver with deep draws on the regulator.

Gradually the boat faded from view, and the lake grew progressively more bleak, its utter sameness mocking his advance, the sunlight filtering through so dimly that only the luminescence of the dials allowed him to read the gauges at all. The murky water reminded him of the Pacific after a storm had churned up the bottom, but it lacked the ocean's vitality of kelp, waves, and sealife—nothing here but opaque gloom that went on and on.

Yet he felt so alive, so charged up, and turned on. . . .

At twenty-five feet he adjusted the buoyancy-compensator vests and leveled out for a straight course to the center of the dam's face, staying well above the decompression limit of thirty-three feet, concentrating on the gurgle of rising bubbles which had for him the sound of a laughing, applauding crowd—a horde of people urging him on against the odds.

When the elapsed time indicated the halfway point, he felt a slackening of apprehension, a relaxation of his jaw muscles clenching on the mouthpiece, but still his peace of mind was tainted by a marginal doubt that in striking out on a rough compass heading, he had gone astray from the most direct route to the dam and compromised his chances of intercepting it on center. A glimpse over his shoulder assured him that the bomb was gliding majestically along on its leash, resembling a sleek gray dolphin accompanied by a pair of bass acting as pilot fish.

The surface of the water glowed with the wan light of a recessed candle flame viewed through a side of thick wax, and in trying to ignore it he felt the reverse of the uneasiness about altitude that forbids the mountaineer to look down. He was afraid to look up! He kept thinking that if the river were at its natural level—its soon-to-be-restored level—his present height above the canyon floor would put him soaring through the air.

His sinuses and throat were beginning to chafe from the dryness of the compressed air, and his feet were going numb from the cold—signs which normally prompted him to surface. But today he had a purpose, and the discomfort merely seemed to enhance the drama of his effort.

He passed a clump of algae that floated in lethargic suspension, its outshoots weaving like jellyfish tendrils in a passive search for sustenance. Checking his watch, he saw that he was eight minutes overdue, which meant that his compass heading was considerably in error or that irrespective of his admonitions to the contrary Lisa had let him off well before the three-hundred-yard buoy line.

Doubling the present overtime to account for the return trip would leave him dangerously short of air, so he was compelled to consider leaving the bomb immediately and heading back to the boat. But somehow he could not take the risks seriously. Despite his dutiful caution he felt fundamentally charmed today, immune to harm, destined to succeed. . . .

And indeed, charmed he was. For suddenly looming out of the muck a dozen feet ahead was the towering verticle face of the dam, eliciting from him a gay grin with little bubbles of air escaping from the corners of his mouth like a fleet of balloons released in celebration.

With the wary respect of a hunter for his quarry he propelled himself ahead and ran a gloved hand over the expanse of concrete, envisioning how beautifully the beast would go down. For a few yards he finned along parallel with the face, triumphing in its immensity. Then jovially chiding himself for wasting vital air, he set to work unhooking the seventy-pound weight belt which was strapped like an anchor around the bomb. He fed it down into the depths by slipping its three hundred feet of attached rope, coil by coil, off the end of the pipe. Exhausting a small volume of air from the vests would make the weighted bomb negatively buoyant and would cause it to sink until the weights touched bottom, stopping the bomb's descent and leaving it positioned three hundred feet above the river bottom like an inner tube tethered by a rope to a sunken rock.

With the release of the final coil he swam forward and unleashed the watercycle from the bomb. A second small control lever on the valve regulated the exhaust, and by pushing the lever he released a jet stream of gas, causing the bomb to nose dive toward the rope of weights, gently beginning to sink.

Vaguely troubled by the profusion of bubbles, he waved them aside and saw with incredulous panic that the lever had remained depressed! The air was continuing to gush from the vests; the bomb would sink straight to the bottom instead of stopping at its proper height where the dam would be thin enough to break.

Frantically he darted beneath the bomb, furiously kicking to maintain it aloft until he could free the frozen control lever. But his efforts failed, and the bomb continued to plummet, the water streaming against the bottom of his face mask, threatening to dislodge it. He reached out for the watercycle to gain its additional power, but already it was a blurred shadow mocking him from above in serene solitude.

Working his jaw to equalize the pressure in his ringing ears, he gave the lever a final yank, and when it failed to yield, released his hold on the bomb.

Unexpectedly he was torn by the shoulders and flipped onto his back with an impact that knocked the breath from his lungs. Madly swirling around some hidden pivot point, he was dragged down through the darkening reservoir. Blindly he lashed out to free himself and struggled to discover where his airtanks had become snagged, but the water was soon pitch black, a closed coffin. A scream rose in his throat against the tide of gulped air, his mind fighting a fog of panic and nitrogen narcosis, a mass exodus of reason under raging terror.

Overhead his finned feet whirled like the blades of a ceiling fan, and the vessels in his temples throbbed as if to burst. Fitfully he curled into a fetal position and groped for purchase on the bomb, tears of fright mingling in his mask with leaking water, which he attempted to expell with violent snorts.

At last his fingers succeeded in searching out one of the vests, and spasmodically he grabbed hold of its tubing, pulling it toward him until he felt the valve, then twisting himself around in a crouch until he had managed to work the valve down between his heels.

With his final reserves of strength he began to straighten his legs, using the full power of his thighs on the frozen control lever.

Give, you son-of-a-bitch, he prayed. *My god, give, give, give . . .*

It gave—snapping up all at once.

He stabbed at the inflation lever and wept at the sound of gas rushing from the pipe's own small air-tank into the buoyancy-compensator vests, slowing the bomb's descent and finally stopping it altogether.

Almost against his will he looked at the dial of his depth gauge. One hundred and eighty-eight feet below the surface.

Shivering violently and clenching the regulator in his teeth, he sloughed the straps of his tank harness and felt for the snag on the nylon rope, which was held taut by the pressure of the diving weights three hundred feet below. A cloud of dizziness enveloped him as he attempted to undo the snarl, and in a moment of involuntary refuge he envisioned himself safely on shore at the marina but was jarred back to awareness by an awful ringing in his ear, followed by a searing, unrelenting pain, like a grain of sand on a cornea, which continued to worsen until he tasted blood at the back of his palate and realized with dazed horror that an eardrum had ruptured.

The waters swirled. He felt as if he were locked in a churning clothes washer, his sense of direction evanesced. Convulsively he vomited in the water, choking on water gulped back into his throat while gasping for air. Feeling increasingly groggy, increasingly confused, he was hazily aware that he had somehow managed to free his tanks from the rope, but he was unclear about his next step, his mind losing track of time and drifting toward sleep as if bored with the struggle for survival.

So this was how it would end. . . . He felt only an abstract curiosity about his own death, noting how calming it was to be utterly bereft of hope.

But no one will know! he thought with a small revival of alarm. He would die without witness and pass unnoticed!

The water in his eustachian tube was slowly warming from the heat of his body, his balance beginning to return. Fervently he made a sacrificial promise that if he survived this, he would never again scuba, never even enter the water. And on those terms he became convinced that he would escape this tight spot just as he had escaped others. But a spiteful, malicious part of his mind reminded him that all dead men had made it—until the end.

At this depth he was using his air at five times the normal rate, making it impossible for him to await the full return of his balance. So taking his direction from his rising bubbles and reshouldering his tanks, he drew a few final breaths before beginning his ascent.

With a silent cry of rage and desperation he froze as his regulator began to honk, signaling the end of his air. He visualized himself attempting a free ascent of one hundred and ninety feet without decompression, saw embolisms exploding his lungs in bloody masses.

The honk faded. The air was gone.

He dropped his weight belt and started up—and then with a surge of sudden insight he somersaulted back to the bomb, sought out the air tank which fed the buoyancy-compensator vests, and held his breath while unhooking the tank from the valve and connecting it to his regulator. With hoarse, ratchety sobs, he sucked in the air, and when his pulse had calmed, he unshouldered his own empty tanks and unleashed the straps of the smaller one from the bomb.

Again he started up, finning like a windup water toy with the fresh tank dangling from his shoulder. Mechanically he matched his speed to that of his rising bubbles, drowsily exhorting himself to maintain the regulation sixty feet per minute and to ignore the sense of panic which urged speed. Against all instinct he continuously exhaled, humming aloud to insure a constant flow of pressurized gas from his lungs.

He moved blindly in the abyss with only periodic orientation to the surface, occasionally raising a hand to feel for the direction of his bubbles, until his outstretched fingers abruptly smashed a solid obstruction.

Immediately he jammed the regulator in his mouth
and felt for the obstacle which seemed to be heavy,
metal mesh—possibly a trash guard for one of the
dam's vertical intake towers, which meant that he had
been swimming on an angle to the horizontal when he
rammed it. But now he had a sure way up to the light,
and while keeping a hand lightly along a rod, he re-
sumed his ascent, the first faint glow of sun in the
water overhead warming him like a blazing fire, revealing what was indeed the round, striated wall of a
tower rising like a monolith toward the surface.

He rose steadily, then paused for a decompression
stop at twenty-five feet, and again at ten. Clinging to
the mesh, he breathed from the tank and guessed at
the time required. He knew that too short a decompression would endanger his life, but knew too that
the tank would not support more than a few minutes.

Gradually he had begun to notice a small itch in his
right knee, symptomatic of an errant bubble of nitrogen expanding in the joint, possibly permanently dam-
aging the tissues. But the crippling of a limb now
seemed a trivial concern, and when the airtank finally
failed, he abandoned it on the wire mesh and finned
straight up, prodded by a sudden onslaught of claus-
trophobic terror.

As his head broke the water's surface, he inhaled
the clear, moist air with voracious greed, fighting the
drowsiness that threatened with each fresh lungful to
overcome him entirely. The pain of his ruptured eardrum was his only hold on sobriety.

He kept his face close to the wire mesh with his

mouth just clearing the water and hoped that his black wet suit hood would be taken for a bit of wood bumping against the trash guards. In his minimal survey he saw that he was on the south side of the Arizona tower and that directly above his head was the bridge walkway connecting the top of the tower to the sidewalk which ran along the summit of the dam.

Off to his right the tower was in shadows, and he began to inch his way toward the darkness, keeping his back to the dam and submerging at the outcropping sections to pull himself along underwater.

Well hidden in the shadows and enclosure of the columns, he surfaced on the tower's northeast side. The pain in his knee had worsened, and he knew that the presence of any additional bubbles in his bloodstream could kill him. But checking his watch, he realized that he would likely die anyway, since the bomb was set to go off in half an hour—timed, in a flash of unthinking optimism, for the last few minutes of daylight so he could watch the unfolding of its splendors.

The yellow boat seemed to hover like a setting sun at the world's edge, emitting irregular glints of light which he took to be reflections from Lisa's telephoto lens scanning the water for some sign of him. But as he leaned out beyond the projection of a rib to catch her attention, he noticed a guard strolling along the walkway of the tower, indifferently gazing down at the lake. Quickly Phillip clamped the snorkel bit in his teeth and submerged, clinging to the hope that Lisa had already spotted him and that she would be inspired to some insanely heroic effort, like getting the

boat over the cable to rescue him. But despite the notion's appeal, somehow he knew that she had not and
that his only hope lay in regaining his wind and
sprinting for the boat, seizing the advantage of surprise from the untended coast guard cutter.

Upright along the grill, he bobbed like flotsam with
the shallow waves, sedated by the lulling security of
having made it to the surface, his mind leaping skittishly away from any thoughts of the bomb, as if reluctant to embrace terror again quite so soon. The
pain in his knee was sending a taproot down his calf
with offshoots up his thigh, feeding on his strength
like a rapacious weed, and he kept the limb bent at an
angle while the nerves slowly went numb with fatigue.

Carefully he poked the upper half of his head above
the water and saw that the guard had moved away
and that the yellow boat was approaching him along
the buoy line. And despite his certain knowledge that
Lisa could never succeed in jumping the cable, he
cherished an hysterical belief in her power to accom-
plish the impossible. But when the boat was directly
in line with the tower, the squared-off stern swung
into view and then diminished as it pulled away, leaving him alone. At the periphery of his terror over
being abandoned was a small lump of gratitude that
she had waited until the last possible moment before
going.

Seven minutes remained before the blast.

With forced composure he put his facemask underwater and reached down to unhook the straps from
his heels, noting with wry irony that the fins, which

were advertised as floatable, immediately sank. He jammed the toes of his neoprene boots into the holes of the grating and pulled himself fully out of the water, climbing the mesh up the side of the tower.

An answering clamor of alarm and the rumbling of boat engines sounded from somewhere behind him.

His arms trembled under the strain of supporting his weight between steps, the bad leg nearly useless now, a burden to be carried. He glanced to his rear and saw half a dozen boats bounding over the water with aimed rifles at their bows, and he felt chilled by the possibility that those idiots might get hold of him and drag him into one of their death boats.

In a spray of water they halted at the base of the tower and shouted at him over a bullhorn. A man in a fishing cap that was pinned with flies grabbed at the grating, his eyes burning with excitement and hunger, his mouth a black, screaming hole of anger. Along the top of the dam a second group of men rushed toward the walkway of the intake tower as if to cut Phillip off from the top. But he continued to climb, resolved to escape the water at any cost.

Suddenly the grating quivered as the man in the cap started up after him, and with the last of his strength Phillip dragged himself the remaining five feet, over the wall of the tower's lowest bacony to throw himself face down on the concrete floor.

Drawing pistols, the group of men on the highway charged across the tower's bridge walkway, and within seconds he heard their steps thundering down the interior stairway and felt the vibrations of their attack in his cheeks and chest.

Through closed eyelids he saw a sudden flash of light that was so brilliant it made him scream in pain, followed by a roar that seemed to split his flesh, to flay his muscles and gouge his raw nerves. He was lifted bodily with a force that squeezed the breath from his lungs like juice from a lemon, and he opened his eyes to see himself invisibly pinned by a hurricane wind to the balcony railing two feet above the floor, which trembled convulsively, marbling with hairline cracks before sections of it seemingly exploded into nothingness. A howling gale of water and debris raged by at arm's reach, putting him in the saving shadow of the tower, and he knew that if he had been a few feet to the right or left, he would be suffering the full violence of the blast.

Abruptly, a jet stream of water shot up from the lake, carrying the boats aloft like so many Ping-Pong balls. The coast guard cutter rode to a height of eighty feet before tumbling off into the spray, and the rowboats split apart as if glued with honey, leaving **the men** to awkward hundred-foot cannonball dives which were divested of any dignity by their certain failure.

Overhead the jet flattened like a column of batter hitting an inverted griddle in a fluffy pancake of steam. The fury abated as suddenly as it had begun, succeeded by a heavy fog as enveloping as thick syrup, the quiet disturbed by a headless torso that parted the mist in the dispirited free-fall of a nightmare apparition.

Freed from the wind's pressure, Phillip slipped down along the balcony rail, then crawled to the door of an interior stairway and tried to open it. But it was torqued on its hinges, wedged immovably in its frame. For a moment he considered leaping over the railing into the mist, down into the waters of Lake Mead that were surging through the unseen hole in the dam. But he had never really been one to go down with the ship, nor a romantic who indulged in senseless gestures, so he stood upright and found that he had to lean on an angle. The tower was sharply tilted from the vertical.

Looking at its cracked shell with fresh wonder at his own good fortune, he saw that it would be possible to scale it from the outside, like climbing a slide from the bottom. With a toe of his boot stuck into one of the concrete's jagged clefts, he located a handhold in a crack and slowly began to inch his way toward the walkway level of the tower, unable to see whether its bridge to the dam remained passable, and not much caring.

The fog's lacy fingers swirled around him, caressing the black skin of his wet suit with intimate, approving strokes. He moved like a man in love, until his hand struck something soft and he discovered the legs of a body that was wedged into a crevice of the upper balcony as tightly as a pimento in an olive. He climbed over the railing, ripped a tube of denim from a jean leg, and folded it into a mask for his mouth as a filter against the low level radiation particles.

Continuing on, he was carried by a welling of personal triumph, an ecstasy so pure that he could not look beyond the present moment of savoring his success. He had done it! It was over! No one could force the turtle back in its shell. Was it possible that his mother's wedding bouquet would end up in Tijuana?

He stumbled over what turned out to be the severed end of an automobile. Noting the New Mexico license plate with its motto *Land of Enchantment,* he smiled to himself behind the denim mask.

And then he saw the walkway stretching ahead out of the mist, damaged but passable, and he knew with certainty that today he was indeed blessed by fate.

THIRTEEN

Leaning on a supply closet shelf full of boxed soap and toilet paper, John tried to clear his mind in the only quiet place he had ever discovered at the bureau. During the last seventy-six hours he had slept only eight, and it looked as if it would be many hours more before he slept again. His first reaction to the news of the Hoover blast had been a decision to move. He reasoned that if Lisa was capable of blowing up a dam, she was capable of seeking him out for revenge, and the fear added to the guilt he felt over the horror to be faced by the victims' families, their suffering caused, at least in part, by his own negligence in letting Lisa slip through his hands.

For a moment he closed his eyes and pillowed his head on a roll of paper towels, then jerked upright to keep from falling asleep. He was dying to go home to bed, but it would be hours yet before he could leave. He opened the closet door and passed into the snack room. After checking through the venetian blinds to see whether the sun had finally risen, he backed through the task force center's door carrying a cellophane-wrapped doughnut and the only soda left

in the machine. The center was overcrowded with
fifty-odd agents shouting to be heard in the stuffy,
forty-foot-square room crammed with desks, telephone lines, and movable file carts. A bank of bulletin
boards had been set up by the door. In one of the
washed-out photos the single remaining intake tower
of Hoover was seen to be twisted askew like the prong
of a fork caught in a garbage disposal, but the dam
itself was holding, and the water level of the lake was
undiminished.

With an aching in his throat John looked over the
list of dead and injured, which had swelled now to
over a hundred, and he ignored the censuring look of
one of the older men and escaped to an office that
had been emptied of its desks and chairs to furnish
the task force center.

As he sat on the floor and took a swallow of the
Orange Crush, his teeth fairly peeling at its sweetness,
his eyes strayed to a tacked-up reproduction of one of
the photos of Lisa Ferro he had taken from her apartment. Yesterday it had made the back pages of a few
local newspapers in connection with a story on missing "materials" at Consolidated Atomic, but today it
would probably appear on every front page in the
world. The only other photograph of her that had
turned up so far was useless for identification, an un-
derexposed, sixth-grade snapshot which showed a
braces-strewn grin and curly, naturally blond hair.
There was no resemblance to Lisa as an adult—though
if one believed the testimony of the childhood playmate who had provided it and that of the people who
had known Lisa during her high school years in Long

Beach, the bureau was misguided in looking for her at all, since Lisa was apparently the sweetest little cupcake ever to pop from an oven, loved and approved by all who had sampled her. Repeatedly the agents conducting the interviews had been castigated for even suspecting her of the bombing; Lisa, the superior student, responsible babysitter, and volunteer candy striper, who had never been charged with as much as a traffic violation. Stranger still was the recurring misunderstanding that Lisa had died a few years before, a rumor that the bureau was still tracking down.

Posted on the wall beside the photo was a memo recounting what little the survivors of the blast had reported on their sightings of a man in a wet suit climbing an intake tower: a Caucasian male, between five-feet-ten and six-feet-two, ranging in weight from one hundred and sixty to one hundred and ninety pounds. A description that narrowed the number of suspects to twenty million.

The memo went on to report another intriguing tale, the story of a teen-age boy who had spotted an unmanned boat racing away from Boulder Beach well after the atomic blast. It had been watched by a woman, partially concealed in some brush, who had disappeared when the boat burst into flames about two miles from shore. But the boy maintained an adolescent's vivid impression of her—"Long black hair. Big tits and ass. A wop or wetback. An older woman—about twenty-five."

The boy had not had a clear view of the woman's face, but was positive that she bore no facial resemblance to Lisa Ferro or Mary Rose Stoval and was certain that her outfit was not a disguise. Considerably more vague about the boat, he was confident only of its color, yellow and white, probably a twenty-four-foot cabin cruiser—a description which fit the Vegas office's log entry on a vessel that had been seen near the buoy line about fifteen minutes prior to the blast. According to their report a pair of agents in an outboard had struck up a short conversation with the passenger aboard the boat and presumably had been confident it was not Lisa Ferro. But both men had been killed in the blast, so it was impossible to know for sure.

After making certain that his office door was closed, John removed a small hip flask of Scotch from his jacket and sought the only relaxation he was likely to get for the next few days, trying to block out the angles, theories, logistics, and plans. With a sense of defeat he wondered what it would be like to be one of the millions who knew nothing more than what they read in the papers and who were free to escape the memory of the blast by going to the movies or playing poker with friends. Perhaps, he thought, instead of entering the bureau after law school he ought to have taken a shot at a practice. And by now he might be raking in the money by handling the easy cases like collections, divorces, and personal injury—except that nothing made his head ache like the sight of a blue-backed interrogatory.

He took another sip from the flask and thought about prying free half an hour to meet Colleen for breakfast at Ship's coffee shop, hesitating only because he knew that she would drive him crazy by trying to dig out an inside track on the Hoover story.

At the sound of approaching footsteps he capped the flask and dropped it back into his suit jacket pocket.

The door was opened by the newest agent in the office, a UCLA law graduate who wore his hair in a Clint Eastwood pompadour and seemed on the verge of inducing a carcinoma of the vocal cords by forcing his naturally high voice down to the raspy depths of his hero's.

"Dr. Bennett's going to be here in about twenty minutes," he told John, speaking in soft conspiracy, probably smelling the alcohol and wanting credit for his magnanimity in letting it slide. Ever since news of the blast he had been paying homage to John's celebrity in being the only agent to have known their most wanted fugitive, his absurd deference implying that John's girl had done him proud by making the big time.

"Do you want to talk in here?" asked the agent. "It's a madhouse everywhere else."

"Fine. Would you bring us some chairs?"

"Sure." He depressed his voice to new depths of man-to-man confidentiality. "Did you hear about the fingerprints at Ferro's apartment?"

"What about them?"

"They don't match her records."

"How can that be?"

The agent shrugged. "We're running them through the computer now."

"Well, let me know the minute you hear."

The agent nodded and left the room, and John checked his pocket directory under RAM Corp, then picked up the telephone and called Dr. Lewis at home.

Lewis's voice was groggy with sleep, closer to croaks than human speech. Quickly John explained that he needed some answers on the Hoover blast; and to his relief Lewis was eager to offer assistance.

"We're all in this together," said Lewis, brushing aside John's apology for the early call. "How can I help?"

John briefed him on the damage at Hoover and explored the possibility that one of the terrorists had climbed an intake tower in a wet suit before the blast. "The area is still highly radioactive, so we haven't made a thorough search. But the body hasn't shown up in the aerial photos, and we're wondering if it's possible that he could have gotten out of there alive."

Lewis was silent so long that John was afraid that he had drifted back to sleep, but finally he managed to rouse himself and to answer, in a voice that was full of effort, with a lecturer's automatic authority.

"According to the Bikini study some of the people on the ships wouldn't have been incapacitated right away." He spoke in a monotone, then paused as if to await another question before continuing. "If your man were right in the shadow of the blast, down in the trough of the tower and railing, he might have been spared the shock wave and flying debris that caused most of the deaths. In Hiroshima the bomb was forty times more powerful than this one, but a small percentage of the people survived within a thousand feet of point zero."

John was beginning to feel the Scotch; he was careful to enunciate. "You're estimating this one at half a kiloton?"

"Somewhere in that range." Lewis sounded sad, and John was relieved there was no note of wanting credit for having predicted the disaster. "They'd have needed at least a full kiloton to breach the dam. Not getting a tidal wave in Lake Mead makes me think they had a low yield, but it was still big enough not to be called a fizzle."

"Okay," said John. "Let's assume this guy survived the blast and that his wet suit protected him somewhat from a drenching of radioactive water. I still don't see how he could walk away after breathing the mist."

"Well, certainly there'd be a probability of lung damage." Lewis was so blasé he might have been predicting a spring shower. "Radiation sickness would set in within a couple minutes, but any skin damage would depend on how much water got through the opening of the suit. At the very least he'd have burns on his face, but those would disappear in a few days. If he managed to walk away, I'd guess he got an exposure of three hundred to a thousand rems—which means he could go into a latent period for a few weeks where all his symptoms disappear and he feels rather well."

"Would he be active?"

"Yes. . . ." There was a pause as Lewis shifted his weight in bed. "Then in three weeks or so he'd begin to lose hair, hemorrhage under the skin, and maybe to bleed internally. If he survived three or four months without succumbing to kidney damage, tuberculosis, or infection, he'd probably make it."

John sighed. He was relieved to hear that the survivors in the hospital who had suffered similar radiation exposure would have a real chance of recovering, but he wanted the son-of-a-bitch who was responsible to die.

After thanking Lewis for his help, he hung up. And with his worst suspicion confirmed, he removed from his pocket a photocopy of the letter that had been taped to the door of the *Los Angeles Times* only hours before by one of the maniacs responsible for the blast. The letter was addressed to Jack Smith, a popular humor columnist who often focused on the everyday mishaps of friends and relatives, and it was written with a flip facetiousness that chilled John every time he read it.

Quickly he skimmed it again to prepare himself for Dr. Bennett's analysis.

Dear Jack,

So sorry to hear of the trouble between your Airedales and Mr. Gomez. Must be a drag to deal with the many pitfalls of your life and still find time to churn out that daily column. So I thought I'd give you a hand by passing along something right up your alley that you could work into a cute misadventures yarn.

Get this: a guy from The Big Orange (how

aptly you tagged Los Angeles, Jack) is going to
Hoover Dam with the nuclear bomb that he built
single-handedly (to be strictly honest he received
minor assistance from his womanfriend, but a little literary license never hurts, does it?), but the
poor guy is absolutely jinxed! He forgets his map,
spills his coffee, and almost runs out of gas. He's
headachy, constipated, and ulcerated. (No of-
fense, Jack, but maybe you could give this part a
kind of Erma Bombeck slant?) And then after
this dispiriting six-hour ride, when they're right
on the goddamn lake, his womanfriend realizes
that the buoys have been moved and decides that
they should call it off at the last minute and go
home!

But our hero is headstrong, Jack, and he's chal-
lenged by a little adversity—all to his huge regret!
The poor fellow gets snagged on his bomb and is
dragged down two hundred feet underwater,
where his air tank promptly runs out and his eardrum ruptures. (And you thought you had problems building a retreat in Baja!)

Then in the best tradition of farce he is forced
to climb up an intake tower with his tail between
his legs, contemplating the stupidity of getting
stuck within the radius of his own blast! (You
could put a funny, fuck-up angle on this, Jack—
like when you wrote about your shutters freezing
up because you used a spray varnish.) But could
you work up a "human" ending? About how he
makes it back to his woman—his wet suit shields
out some of the radiation; he's bumbling, but

charmed, see?—and she gently breaks it to him that all was for naught, that the dam held with only a little drool oozing from its lips.

Well, hope you can fill a few lines with it, Jack—and if it turns out well, maybe I'll contact you for a sequel. (No, I can't reveal it now, but there are countless possibilities; my life is a mine of misadventures lately. I dare say we have a lot in common.)

Fondly,
???????

(Our hero is still nameless. I know you got shafted on credit for naming the Black Dahlia, Jack, so this one is all yours. I rather like "Little Boy"—code name for the lovely we dropped on Hiroshima, but it's not catchy enough, I suppose.)

John folded the letter with a sense of defeat, feeling tainted at being thought attractive by Lisa along with a man of such monstrous aberrancy. And he wondered how he could possibly have missed seeing such gross derangement in her.

With a chair under each arm the new agent showed in Dr. Molly Bennett, a woman in her middle fifties, freckled and hazel-eyed, with short, dark brown hair and a plump figure that was showed to advantage in turquoise sweater and slacks. One of the country's leading criminal psychiatrists, she was a frequent consultant to the bureau. But during their numerous past encounters John had learned that she was shy about renewing acquaintances, habitually hiding behind a businesslike brusqueness which would gradually dissolve as she became immersed in discussion. So he was careful to place the two chairs distant enough that she would not feel her space encroached upon, and he made only minimal small talk as he apologized for awakening her in the middle of the night.

When finally seated, she donned the glasses she had required all along; and at last being able to read his expressions, she began to warm to him.

"They told me you knew the girl he talks about in this letter?" She glanced down at the clipboard on which she carried a copy of the *Times* letter, marked and annotated in her own illegible handwriting.

"Woman, really," said John. "She was twenty-eight."

"And she fooled you?"

He nodded. "At first I was interested in her because I thought she was hiding a fleeing felon we'd been trying to track down. And when I finally realized she was involved in something criminal herself, I put her down as a common thief."

"That's pretty usual; doesn't mean you're not observant. They fool even the professionals." Mechanically she assumed the role of the therapist, reassuring and soothing a client. But as she glanced at her notes, he detected a sudden flatness in her eyes, a look of lameness that he had often felt himself after carefully preparing an analysis and then being forced to go over it all again without that initial, private intensity of formulation.

"Well," she said. "The most obvious characteristic of the letter is that it's written by hand. Your man is being careless; he's giving you clues and wants to be caught. Invariably they do, but first he's going to toy with you a little. Play out the game is how he'd see it. He prides himself on being clever—on taunting and outwitting the authorities."

She watched him nod agreement, then took a deep breath, and he noted how she punctuated her discourse with little physical signs. A breath for paragraphs, a nod for sentences, a blink for commas—a deliberate woman who took care against misunderstanding.

"Okay, that much is obvious," she said. "The brown ink tells me he's seeking distinction—and so, too, the flamboyance of the handwriting and the little pretensions of I *dare say* and *naught*."

Impatiently he craned his neck to get a look at her copy, but her notations were a mystery. "You think he's all pretense? That he's not well-educated?"

"Oh, no—I think he is." Her brows arched for emphasis and he noticed a deep green glint in her eye. "Presumably in the physical sciences to have done what he did. And I'd guess that he has written a fair amount—there's a kind of looseness on paper that comes with practice, not being intimidated by the blank page—which makes me think he's somewhat successful in his profession. His sense of humor about his failure shows he has some objectivity. No hallucinations or delusions, so I'd rule out paranoid schizophrenia. More likely we're dealing with a sadistic sociopath, or psychopath as I still prefer to call them."

"But would a psychopath be this . . ." he fumbled for a word ". . . this *lucid*?"

"Oh, yes. I've known psychopathic professors, doctors, lawyers—and psychologists! To a perceptive eye there's a fundamental maliciousness about them. They are predatory people, but on the surface they can appear utterly normal and rational, and there's a kind of electric aura of energy around them that can be attractive. They have an amazing ability to charm, and often people like them so well that they refuse to testify against them even when they're caught."

John thought of Lisa, of the excitement she aroused in him, the sense of being fully alive, and he recalled with chagrin his confidence at being in control, of leading her into his trap—when it was he who was being led. He noticed Dr. Bennett leaning forward in her chair, studying his face with a concentration that made him uncomfortably aware that he was showing too much.

"The woman bewitched you a little?" She smiled with a mischievousness he hadn't expected from her, a kind of professional delight in her cleverness.

"No, it wasn't that, but she did fool me—"

"She fooled you, *and* she enchanted you! I can see it. You're not a good liar, you know. You hold your hand over your mouth—it's a classic giveaway." Her eyes radiated self-satisfaction and mirth, and he had to laugh in acknowledgment of her perception.

"To me this letter sounds young for some reason," he said, deflecting her attention from himself. "Can you estimate his age?"

"Well, most mass murderers are in their twenties. White and single. But psychologically they're still infantile. Usually they're victims of abuse in childhood, so they're never really civilized or given a conscience. They can't make the progress of healthy children, so they're unhealthy children forever, compulsively seeking the attention they never got from their parents. Morally they're at the level of a baby screaming for care with no anxiety about future punishment."

John thought of the letter's mocking bravado. "You say that he wants to be caught. But doesn't that indicate that he has a conscience?"

She shrugged in dismissal of an insignificant disagreement. "Well, what is conscience anyway? Its accepting a code of mutual respect—a code the psychopath rejects because his childhood proved it worthless. He can't escape his need for love and esteem, and he knows that breaking the law puts him further out on a limb, alienated from society. But what he's desperately seeking in lawlessness is a closeness with people that he never had with his parents. He doesn't fear punishment; he seeks it as a kind of parental discipline—a show of society's love. He wants to be caught because he wants to escape the feeling that no one cares where he is or what he does."

"So you think he'll continue to be careless and to give us clues?"

"Yes, I do." She fidgeted with the clip of the board, snapping it open and closed on her notes. "But the problem here is that he failed in what he set out to do. Psychopaths have an obsessive need to seem successful and worthy of adoration, so he's very dangerous now if he thinks he must succeed before he can allow himself to be caught—as he seems to imply in this bit about a *sequel*. If he runs true to type, he'll be willing to sacrifice everything for a victory over what he sees as the guardians of society."

"Which is us and not Jack Smith, right?"

She smiled. "I'm afraid so."

Absently she glanced at the photograph of Lisa on the wall. "Is that the woman?"

"Yes."

"Very pretty. What a shame . . ."

She was interrupted by a knock on the door, and the agent with the pompadour leaned in, breathless and agitated, beckoning John over.

"We tracked down those death rumors. A psychotherapist named Dr. Lisa Ferro died a few years ago."

"*Dr.* Ferro? How can that be—the same name?" He was struck by a chill of suspicion as he saw a pattern from the past beginning to emerge.

There was a gleam in the agent's eye, the knowing glint of a man about to reveal a punchline. "We got an answer on those fingerprints too."

"And?"

"It's the woman you were looking for, the one who escaped from the Metropolitan Correctional Center in San Diego. Mary Rose Stoval."

FOURTEEN

The compound was in the desert outskirts of Palm Springs, a hundred acres of sand and sagebrush headquartering the Harbor Light, a private halfway house which had been founded for the rehabilitation of drug addicts, but which had become in large part a cultist sanctuary for dropouts from the middle class who were enchanted with each successive pattern in the kaleidoscopic swirl of California thought. About three dozen domes were scattered on the land in no apparent pattern, like a handful of seeds tossed to take root wherever they happened to fall. Most of them had been built by pouring reinforced concrete over mounds of dirt and then digging out the soil to leave the concrete shells. But those fronting on the compound's only expanse of grass—a hundred-foot square crisscrossed with footpaths—were of superior construction and comprised the compound's original, central core. Geodesics shingled with redwood and enlivened with random stained-glass panels, they seemed to be shored up by the buttresses of arching yuccas and cacti encircling their foundation. Outside the garden's rocky borders the sandy dirt showed tracks from a recent raking, its patterns marred where tumbleweeds had blown through.

John walked along a rut in the dirt driveway and looked around for something that resembled an administration building. He had stopped at his apartment for a quick shower and change of clothes before leaving Los Angeles, but the temperature in Palm Springs was soaring into the high eighties, and he felt dirty and exhausted. He paused in front of a structure which was unimaginatively labeled *Food Hut* and watched a tall, obese man with a camera slung around his neck search for a perspective on a group of people who were squatting on the grass in what looked like an encounter group. The man held thick hands in front of him to frame a viewing rectangle and hunched over at the waist with comic diffidence. Then at last he aimed the camera, his elbows lifted high like a bird in flight, and inadvertently he shook the lens each time his meaty finger pressed the shutter button.

The people in the group continued their shrill castigations with none of the usual camera-conscious mugging, primping, or pride. No teeth flashed, no stomachs sucked in, no wide derrières swished out of view. It was as if they had been drained, by identification with the group, of any sense of self. And watching them, John felt chilled by their indifference, thinking he would opt for vain prima donnas any day over these egoless robots.

Distracted by the sound of crumpled paper, he leaned around the curve of the dome to see a woman unloading groceries from a pickup truck, hefting the bag up to her waist on one knee, then taking up some of the weight in her teeth. She kept a second sack at her side in a precarious grip and scurried toward him as if to make the door of the hut before everything crashed around her.

"Need some help?" he asked.

With teeth implanted in the sack she jutted out her chin like a dog offering its ball for a game of fetch, and as he relieved her mouth of its burden, he noticed her pout—a woman who used her vulnerability as a shield. She seemed to be trying to decide if he was friend or foe, but her eyes emptied without conclusion.

"Thanks." She passed in front of him with a slackness to her movements beyond her years. She could not have been much older than he, about thirty-three or thirty-four, but she shuffled into the dome like a woman with five decades of trouble on her mind, her brown hair prematurely streaked with gray and tied in a frumpish braid down her back.

She led the way past a dining area to a quaintly old-fashioned kitchen which took up most of the space of the structure. The dome's struts were visible from the interior like the mammoth skeleton of a prehistoric reptile, covered by a scaly skin of plywood triangles. A few laconic women stood at the counters, chopping, peeling, and beating with the listlessness of survivors of a disaster.

John deposited his sack on a table, and the woman studied him a moment, her mouth set in a line like a slash through an offending phrase.

"I don't remember having seen you here before."
She spoke with the frozen tongue of the intellectually
pretentious, sounding as if it were sutured to the floor
of her mouth.

"I'm with the FBI," he said. "I guess I'm in the
wrong building; I need to see whoever is in charge."

She smiled as if she had caught him in a grammati-
cal error. "If you want to talk about Lisa Ferro, the
one who worked here wasn't the one in the newspapers. She's passed on."

"We're aware of that. Did you know her?"

"Not personally. I'm new here." Her voice dropped
with shyness, as if she viewed her recent arrival as a
charming virginity. He was relieved that he would not
have to question her further.

She volunteered directions to the office of a therapist who had worked with Ferro, and he retreated
outside and began a tortuous path down through the
domes, which were reminiscent of the World War
II Quonset hut barracks he had lived in as a law student. There was the same quality of prevading en-
nui, the same sense of time stopped still by the utter
uniformity of the structures, with none of the symbolic advances and retreats of a mixed neighborhood.
He left the tunnel of domes at a packed-down area
among manzanita bushes and crossed over to enter a
solitary concrete-block structure.

The small waiting room was furnished with a pleasant mixture of rattan furniture and tropical plants, an
optimistic effort to add life to the dull interior.
Through an open door came a male's low voice, with

the pained character of a confession and a touch of caginess in overstating his case for sympathy. Realizing that he had stumbled into the middle of a therapy session, John considered his dilemma: the open door made it impossible to approach with any propriety, but if he were to sit and wait until the session was over, he would be put into the position of an eavesdropper. Uncomfortable with the alternatives, he took a breath and walked over, then stood in embarrassment during a few more seconds of the man's recital before the woman behind the desk finally noticed him.

"Yes?"

"You're Dr. Sloan?"

"That's right."

He was surprised that she was so young, too young to be a therapist. *She looks as if she'd have trouble telling you that your fly is down or that you have lettuce stuck between your teeth,* he thought.

"May I speak to you in private a few minutes?"

"What is it about?" Her voice was middle range and seemed to emanate from the center of her being, with nooks and crannies of hollowness that echoed and enhanced.

He displayed his badge out of range of the man, who had kept his head sheepishly averted, prompting her to move from behind her desk. She wore a loose, floor-length caftan, in keeping with her ethnic appearance, which was Jewish or Italian. Her eyes were compressed almonds, pale green in the sunlight; her hair, dark brown and shoulder-length, slightly waved.

In a subdued conference she bent over her patient, who stood with the alacrity of an employee suddenly granted the afternoon off. With eyes staring directly into John's, as if to deny any embarrassment at having been overheard, he left the room.

She motioned for John to take a seat.

"I didn't mean to break anything up," he apologized.

She smiled. "I think I'm as relieved as he was. Is this about Lisa Ferro?"

"Yes, I understand you worked with her?"

"If you had called, I could have saved you a trip. It's not the same Lisa Ferro."

"Yes, I know. The woman we're looking for called herself Lisa Ferro, but she was impersonating the real one." Explaining a little about the case, he showed her the old prison mug shots of Mary Rose and one of the snapshots of "Lisa" he had found at her apartment. Once again the comparison shocked him; he felt a dull pain at his failing of insight. But it buoyed him somewhat to see that Sloan's incredulity seemed equal to his own.

Looking down at the photos, she shook her head in amazement. "What's uncanny is the expression. The physical resemblance isn't that strong, but she has the same impatience in her eyes and half smile that the real Lisa always had."

John was disarmed by her ready cooperation. Most people were circumspect in discussing anything at all with the bureau, if only as an assertion of their independence. But she seemed to accept him as a fellow professional, and there was just a hint of shyness to her that made him think she'd like to help him with an insight.

"Do you know if Mary Rose was ever a patient of the real Lisa Ferro?" he asked.

"Not here." Sitting on the desk, she crossed her legs, but seemed to feel awkward, so she scooted back and left her feet dangling, swinging them a bit. "It was after Lisa left and went to work at the Metropolitan Correctional Center in San Diego."

He wondered how much she knew. "That's where Mary Rose escaped."

"I know." She looked pleased to be on familiar ground. "I noticed it in the papers."

"You were acquainted with the case?"

"Vaguely." She glanced at her lap and smoothed the folds and wrinkles. "Lisa and I were in school together, and then we both worked here awhile. There weren't many women in our field, so we rooted for each other. We still kept in touch when she went to San Diego. About once a month we'd have a three- or four-hour lunch—lots of coffee and multiple desserts. Pour out weeks of frustration. Neither of us had much confidence back then. If we felt on shaky ground with a patient, we'd discuss it. Lisa did talk about Mary Rose a little, and I have some impressions if it'd be any help."

"Of course." He smiled at her tone of doubt. "It'd be a big help. I'm operating in the dark as far as Mary Rose goes. I knew her as Lisa Ferro, and it's hard to reconcile the two."

She pursed her lips and gave a little shake of her

head, as if trying to clear her mind of surprise. "What I don't understand is how anyone could carry off an impersonation for that length of time without someone finding out."

He shrugged. "A lot of people get away with it. There's no cross-indexing of death and birth certificates, so it's fairly easy if you avoid the person's associates."

Her eyes met his with sly interest. The idea of going underground herself someday intrigued her just a bit. "Did Mary Rose actually try to get work with Lisa's credentials?"

"She set up her own practice." He expected surprise that would mirror his own, but Sloan smiled ironically. In her eyes was a directness he liked, a steadiness that implied that nothing was worth agonizing over. Yet he sensed too that she kept a lid at the other extreme on joy, making for a strange solidness that was relaxing.

She noticed his confusion over her smile. "I'm remembering how Mary Rose liked to get a rise out of Lisa by mimicking anything that sounded like psychological jargon. Lisa said it was eerily accurate when Mary Rose got rolling in the role of therapist. So I can see how someone might just pass her off as a quack without doubting her qualifications."

"She did better than that." Briefly he sketched the stories of former patients who had called the bureau that morning after reading the stories in the papers to tell of being treated by Mary Rose Stoval posing as Dr. Ferro. Uniformly they had been stunned to learn of the deception, never having doubted her credentials and almost unanimously having profited from their sessions with her, testifying to saved lives and enriched marriages. None had viewed her unorthodox methods as disturbing, and all had been inspired by her risk-taking, go-for-broke approach.

"Wow, it makes you wonder," said Sloan, showing her youth with a wryness to her expression. Her face was eminently readable, and he was unaccountably relieved to rid himself of the prejudice that all therapists were as crazy as their patients. It was one of the few pleasures of his job, brightening a day or a week—the discovery of an admirable human being.

She wore a wedding band the thickness of a couple of strands of hair, and it seemed more serious for being understated; a love held private.

When she caught his gaze on her hand, he cleared his throat. "Did you get the impression that Lisa liked Mary Rose at all? That they were close?"

"Not close." She was quick to correct. "Lisa could never break through her defenses. But she liked her; Mary Rose made a great impression. She was affable and witty—very charming until Lisa would start probing her background. Then she'd cut her off—or lie outrageously. She never believed her own lies, she just liked toying with Lisa. She had an instinct for knowing exactly what people wanted to hear. Insight into everyone but herself."

"So I noticed."

She smiled at his self-mocking tone. "One thing that really sticks in my mind is the way she'd tell Lisa that she'd always been a happy person, that she loved to get up in the morning and see what the day would bring."

He thought of the blasted intake towers and the list of dead and injured. "What could twist a person so badly? Do you know anything about her history?" ·

Her head dropped in a wistful curve into the past, looking for impressions buried beneath the dust of time. "I don't think anyone really knows what happened. Not even Mary Rose. Her mother left her when she was very young, and she idealized her father even though he probably beat her. As a kid she was constantly being admitted to hospital emergency rooms with bruises or broken limbs."

He couldn't reconcile the horrific background with the radiant face he had known. The story irritated him somehow. "What do you mean *idealized*? Why didn't someone do something?"

"Oh, they did. They patched her up and sent her home." There was a bite to her voice that managed to skirt bitterness, a story too old and familiar to evoke outrage. "As far as denying any problem with her father, that's pretty common when the anger goes deep enough. There's a subconscious fear that the rage can burn one alive."

He closed his eyes a moment and tried to rub away the beginnings of a headache in his temple. He wanted to sleep, to forget all this. Instead he moved forward on his chair to remain alert. "Did Lisa ever try to worm the truth from the father?"

Sadness made a thin slash of her mouth. "He committed suicide while Mary Rose was still in high school. I think her first episode of impersonation was about a year after his death." She squinted in thought, sorting out her recollections. "One of her teachers was killed in a car accident, and Mary Rose got a job at a private grammar school using the woman's professional history—which she had gotten by breaking into the school's files. She was found out a few weeks later, but the school didn't have any complaints about her teaching. Apparently the kids loved her."

John felt queasy, alternating between anger at Mary Rose for not finding another outlet and pity for the battered little girl inside who wanted revenge. "How do you explain the impersonations? It seems a bizarre solution."

"I don't know—denial, escape . . ." She looked abashed, as if her lack of experience in general were being rammed home. "I've never handled an impersonator. It's very rare. But as far as the literature goes, the impersonation of professionals is a common choice —the Hillside Strangler was impersonating a therapist at some point, I think. In fact I think one of his victims was a client. For a bright sociopath like Mary Rose a therapist's authority and status could have been inviting camouflage. My guess is that her self-esteem was so low, she chose to abandon her personality and make a fresh start. Battered children are usually consumed with self-contempt."

He fumbled to make sense of his confusion. "Would she know what she was doing?"

Sloan pulled at a thin strand of hair, absently running her fingers down its length. "Oh, probably. But it's like a kid's game of imaginary playmates. They know their playmate isn't real, but the truth is irrelevant to their needs."

She looked down at the two photos, shifting her gaze back and forth between them. Her interest seemed clinical now; she had gotten over her surprise and was looking for the key to the puzzle. "I'd guess that the enormous weight loss shows an obsessive need to change. She became Lisa right down to her eating habits. Presumably she'd have preferred to be thinner before, but she didn't have the self-discipline until she became someone else."

He shook his head. Some element of pure, inexplicable evil seemed to be missing, and he found himself recoiling from the implicit sympathy of understanding. He sighed. "I guess this is one of those freakish things no one ever understands."

She smiled sympathy for his cynicism. "You're forgetting the California factor."

"What's that?"

Her eyes were bright and self-mocking. "Lisa and I devised it to account for the gaps. It's what makes people with just regularly awful backgrounds explode out here—the lack of pressure that blows the lid off, so to speak."

"Don't get too technical."

She laughed, then rushed ahead, as if wanting to make sure he took her point somewhat seriously. "The problem is there aren't any excuses in California—no traditions, or oppressive weather, or extended families to hold people back. So it's easy for someone who's unstable to go a little wild trying to be special in a place where conformity and mediocrity aren't enough.

Everything seems possible, so people take their best shots. And some people's shots are lethal."

He thought of all the Village crazies, the kid who talked to windows and the one who preached about an imminent invasion from outer space. "We certainly seem to get more than our share."

"Of course it works the other way." She seemed wary of being overly negative. "For healthy people it's liberating."

John was struck by a sudden thought. "Is it possible that Lisa might have concealed Mary Rose after her escape out of respect for a professional relationship?"

Emphatically Sloan shook her head. "I might, but not Lisa. Too moralistic. She left here because she couldn't relate to the type of patients we got back then—mostly drug addicts and thieves. At MCC it was even worse. She went to San Francisco and got into a group practice."

"That would have been shortly before she died?"

"Maybe six months. She was mugged on Christmas Eve. Robbed and shot with a .22 caliber pistol."

FIFTEEN

Behind the oven's glass the patties lay as flat as poker chips. Giving up hope, she opened the door to slide out the sheet and flipped one of the cookies into a heavy lump on the counter, where she cooled it with her breath until feeling light-headed.

Doubtfully she sampled a bite, then spit the offending mouthful into the garbage disposal, which she filled with the rest of the failed batch. Removing the dessert plate from the dinner tray and spreading out the sandwich and salad to compensate, she added a yellow linen napkin and in a moment of whimsy a bud vase of pansies.

Still, it wasn't much of a meal for the celebration of a miracle: the miracle of Phillip's being alive at all. She had found him limping down a dirt road, shivering without his wet suit, which he had ditched as soon as he was upwind of the radioactive fallout. Utterly dejected over their failure to breach the dam, his attitude had reminded her of their first meeting, the only other time he had been as surly and withdrawn.

Through a remarkable twist of fate he had stumbled into her office seeking psychological counseling, but had routinely denied that there was anything much wrong—just that he couldn't sleep, couldn't eat, couldn't stand to be alone.

With sympathetic encouragement the reasons had emerged: a childhood history that was a nightmare of sadistic neglect. In a calm voice that had chilled her blood he had discussed the burden he had been for his parents, who had coped by denying his presence. He was never touched except in moments of anguish or rage. Servants bathed, dressed, and fed him. His mother professed to love him but spoke to him only out of absolute necessity and only about his immediate needs for food, clothing, and education. Neither of his parents commented on his behavior, either in praise or scorn; his father spoke of him as "the child" and addressed him less than a dozen times in their short acquaintance.

Once banished to a military academy, he was sent a minimal personal allowance despite his parents' enormous wealth. Among Beverly Hills students dressed in outfits from Gucci's, Magnin's, and Saks, he was stigmatized by threadbare clothing and excluded from the expensive extracurricular activities. He sought refuge in studying, but his outstanding grades were unacknowledged even though the school mailed a report to his parents every semester.

But as an adult he remained convinced that they had not particularly wronged him and that he had no real reason to complain. Why then did he fantasize about massive destruction? Why was he so consumed with rage that he plotted the building of bombs?

Lisa's interest had been piqued by the mention of a

homemade atomic bomb. Surely such a thing was an impossibility, wasn't it? He could never make a feasible design, nor obtain the necessary funds, nor avoid blowing himself up during construction—could he? Reluctantly he admitted that his obsession had already reached the point that he had been driven to solve most of the theoretical problems.

Gently assuring him that a professional therapist would be shocked by nothing, she gradually got him to talk about the details and to see that self-acceptance was healthy, that his abilities demanded expression, and that his talents might well result in strange manifestations that were no less valid for being unusual.

After several sessions she had revealed her diagnosis that he was in fact a psychopath who had all the breed's characteristic lust for action—actually quite a common condition among successful professionals like himself. Had he never heard of the Nobel-Prize-winning biochemist in Beverly Hills who was notorious for torturing his research animals and assaulting his poorer students?

Once loosened up, Phillip had knocked Lisa out with his energy, as if she had tapped the core of his being with all its hidden springs of passion and vitality. And gradually she had noticed that she no longer related to him as a therapist, but as an accomplice. Counseling had started to pale in the light of his revelations; she had grown tired of listening to neurotics all day, people so deadly dull that she thought they would be better off satisfying their passion for suicide. So she had abandoned her practice in order to join him in the pursuit of his dream and had never looked back.

Rain was splattering on the patio as she carried the supper through the living room, upstairs to the master bedroom where Phillip languished against a buttress of pillows, looking grim and deflated as he surveyed Tuesday's *Times*. The folded-over front page showed aerial photos of the dam intact, the intake tower alone distorted by the blast.

"You didn't need to bring that—I was going to come downstairs." He kept his eyes on the page and spoke louder than usual to compensate for his ruptured eardrum.

She straddled his legs with the bedtray and tried not to notice the little flaking sores on his forehead or the burns around his mouth and chin. Suspiciously he eyed the sandwich, then deigned to scoop out a fingerful of tuna fish, which he nibbled with indifference.

"Did you call my office?"

"Uh huh." She pushed the salad toward him, knowing he probably wouldn't even try it. Her culinary efforts were barely edible under ordinary circumstances and certainly nothing to tempt an ill man who had already lost nearly ten pounds from lack of appetite. She noticed little flecks of dirt on the lettuce and thought belatedly that she ought to have washed the greens.

"You tell them I was sick?" he asked belligerently.

"Yes sir, boss man!" she snapped, and she was pleased to wring from him a reluctant smile. Knocking sharply on the back of the newspaper, she said, "That Jack Smith thing was a pretty dumb stunt, Phillip."

"Oh . . . you read it?"

"What'd you think? That I wouldn't read the paper or listen to the radio? If you have to show off again, will you please do it in front of *me*? Bragging is how every dumb asshole gets caught."

"I know. . . . It was stupid. . . ." But his smart-aleck grin betrayed something more akin to pride than humility. "I'm sorry about that, Mary Rose."

She snatched the paper and glared at a mug shot accompanying a story that revealed her identity as Mary Rose Stoval.

"Those damn prison photos," she complained. "The stupid shits used a wide-angle lens, and my nose looks like a fat pickle!"

"I think it's flattering, actually."

"Gee, thanks." She felt her nose with her fingers and showed him her profile. "It doesn't look like that now, does it?"

"It's perfect, Mary Rose."

Somewhat mollified, she threw the paper to the floor. "I really *hate* that name, you know. When I told you about it you promised never to bring it up again. Isn't your word even good for a lousy year?"

"I'm not bringing it up. Complain to the L.A. *Times*, Mary Rose."

"Goddamn it, I *mean* it! You promised! I'll never tell you a secret again."

"Okay, okay. . . ." And then in a low aside, as if unable to resist, "Miss Stoval."

She flounced from the bed toward the door, but he called after her, entreating her to return with promises to stick with "Lisa." And finally she conceded, though maintaining her sullenness to drive home her point. She sat on the edge of the bed and began to eat his sandwich and to sip at his tomato juice.

"You should be whoever you like," he said with mock contrition. "Why be bound by birth, right?"

Pissed off by his patronizing, she kept her eyes on the blanket and haughtily said, "I'm a much better Lisa Ferro than the original, you know."

"I'm sure you are."

"You never met her."

"Do I have to see every *Hamlet* to know Olivier is best?"

"Well . . . anyway, I am. She was a real twit, a weak little Milquetoast with barely enough spine to sit upright in a chair. People walked all over her, and she felt guilty that she wasn't as crazy as her patients—though if you ask me, she was neck and neck with a couple of them. Imagine a therapist asking a patient, 'What's your sign?' And she'd actually consult an astrology chart when you'd stump her."

"So why did you become her?"

"Oh, my God," she sighed. Did he know nothing about her yet? Had he spent all this time with her without garnering any clues? She finished off the sandwich and started on the salad, eating around its more loathsome-looking parts.

"So tell me," he persisted. "Am I supposed to read your mind?"

Deliberating a moment, she leaned back on her splayed out arms. "You don't turn down a role just because the current actress doesn't know how to play it."

He smiled. "Then why are you presently passing up the only role in town: Mary Rose Stoval, numero uno on the Ten Most Wanted list, criminal extraordinaire, diabolical mastermind."

She scoffed at his histrionics, but a shy light of interest flickered in her eyes. "Nobody sees me that way. They think I'm some pathetic nut."

"Are you kidding? Nuts can't build nuclear bombs, Mary Rose."

This time she smiled and lowered her face to hide the blush she felt rising in her neck. *Mary Rose Stoval, numero uno. . . .* Was it true?

She set aside the tray and straightened the bedclothes, looking down at him with motherly concern. "Do those radiation burns hurt your lips?"

"They're just cole sores."

Resolved not to challenge his self-deception, she opened the drawer of the nightstand and removed the case containing her otoscope, which she carefully fitted with one of its black cones before removing the sterile dressing from his injured ear.

"Anyway, that's *cold sore*," she said. "You're thinking of *cole slaw*."

"Cold slaw."

Suppressing a grin, she went to wash her hands in the bathroom, then returned and wiped the cone with alcohol. Gently she pulled his ear up and back to provide visualization of the eardrum with its tiny, black blood clots, now healing nicely under her attention.

As she had been doing three times a day, she used an ear-powder blower to dust his ear with a mixture of antibiotic and boric acid powders, then wrapped

his head with a bandolier of sterile gauze, fondly recalling the months she had spent as a general practitioner until forced out by the medical board's goon
squads.

When she had finished the dressing, Phillip flipped
aside the blankets and swung his feet to the floor, revealing the elastic bandage she had used to brace his
knee. He tossed her a yellow quadrille-ruled pad covered with his florid handwriting, and she skimmed the
list he had drawn up.

"A forklift?"

"You can rent that, but buy the air compressor."

"Not me," she said. "If I went out now, I'd be
swamped with paparazzi. I'm a celebrity, remember?"

"So wear your big tits and wig."

As he pulled on some jeans and a shirt, she studied
his face. "Sometimes, Phillip, I think you actually
want us to be caught."

He snatched away the list. "Forget it. I'll do it myself."

"I don't suppose you'd like to forget all this and retire on your money somewhere in Brazil?"

"Getting cold feet?"

"They're frostbitten, gangrenous, and ready to drop
off."

"Well, you'll have to get around on your clay stumps
for a while, because there's no quitting now. That
dam is full of radioactive water."

"Dr. Stoval thinks you're getting a little compulsive—"

"Would you expect me to pass a house of cards and
not want to blow it over?"

"In this case, Phillip, do you really think that hot air will do the trick?"

"Yeah, if it's about ten-to-the-eighth degrees."

"An encore?"

"Sort of. Why not?"

SIXTEEN

Through a café window on the main street of Henderson, Nevada, John watched an agent from the Vegas
office march up the street with a determined, military
stride, his too short slacks flapping at his ankles above
gleaming, spit-shined shoes as he swung into a Standard gasoline station and flashed his badge at the
attendants, making them squirm and defer to his
authority.

With a sigh John turned his back on the scene and
pushed off the café stool, thinking how foolish he had
been to get involved on the level of routine questioning
in this case. Why was he compelled to seek out Mary
Rose directly? *Mary Rose.* . . . How strange it sounded to fasten that mellifluous name to that impudent
face! His image of her smiling brashness was beginning
to fade, making it difficult to remember what part was
real, what part embellishment of a memory. He loathed
what she had done, but his enmity was an act of faith,
and in spite of himself he kept thinking that if he could
see her again, she could explain away her participation.

As he dropped some quarters beside his unfinished
cup of coffee, one of the waitresses caught his eye.

"Sorry we couldn't help," she said.

He shrugged; he hadn't expected success.

Next door he entered a mom-and-pop grocery, his heels aching where the padding of his shoe was wearing off the nails, and he reminded himself to try cushioning them with a layer of folded-up toilet paper. The shelves of the store were tall, and the aisles were narrow with none of the round spy mirrors he so hated. He lingered over a toiletries section, reading labels on shampoo and shaving lotion as he tried to subdue a revulsion against interrogating any more strangers today. The interviews accentuated his shame over letting Mary Rose slip through his fingers, and although it seemed unjustified, he couldn't shake it; there was something fundamentally humiliating about being played for a fool. He had always prided himself on being a good judge of character, but apparently his insights were confined to routine matters.

Realizing that he had exhausted the delays of the toiletries section, he set down a jar of acne cream and proceeded to the counter, where he presented his badge to the kid at the cash register. In a flat monotone he described the yellow boat, then showed the recent photo of Mary Rose.

The boy shook his head, with his greasy hair swinging in an arc across his forehead, his voice bright with expectation. "Nope. Just seen her on television. Any fresh clues?"

Smiling wearily, John summoned all the smartness he could muster. "We're on their trail, son."

Eyes wide, the kid gulped, then gallantly presented John with a candy bar as his own shy contribution to law and order. The Hershey bar was white around the edges with age, and once outside and out of view of the kid John dropped it in a trash barrel. Momentarily he considered sneaking off to a park and taking a much needed catnap, but a vision of Mary Rose hiding out and enduring the terror of being hunted goaded him on.

At the Mobil station next door he displayed the badge and photo to an old man cleaning the window of a pickup truck, but the man barely glanced at them, as if leary of being drawn into contact with the law. Impassively he ran a squeegee along a grimy pants leg and slicked it across the glass.

"Ain't seen her."

"It would have been about a week ago," said John. "Thursday, Friday, or Saturday, probably. Were you working here then?"

"Yep, is this the dam thing?"

John nodded, astonished that there could be any doubt. But he had learned time and again that few people recognized the picture of Mary Rose, either not having read the news or not caring enough to remember.

"Well then, let me see it again. I don't bother with newspapers." The man took the picture in his grease-stained hands and held it carefully along the borders, up close to his eyes and then a little further back, working it into focus. Grunting a few times, he closed his lids as if recalling a scene and then he nodded to himself.

"Yep, she was here all right." He sounded regretful

about becoming involved at all. "With a boy and a boat. Changed clothes in the head."

A primal excitement which John thought had disappeared from his nature welled up with fresh force, and he found himself breathless with anticipation. It was the zeal of a pack dog catching the scent of blood.

"She changed clothes here?" he asked.

"Yep. And if you're lookin' for a dark gal too, that's her." He stabbed at the photo. "Put on a wig and stuff. Looked like a real freak." He stepped aside to allow the pickup truck to drive ahead, then he leaned against the gas tank.

"Was her figure different?" asked John.

The man molded gargantuan breasts and hips in the air. "Jugs like mountains. Guess I should of thought something about it, but I see all kinds of sideshows here. Men looking like women; women like men. Who's got time to care, you know what I mean?"

"You're sure about the boat?"

"Yellow and white, twenty-four footer. Wanted one like it all my life, but never could afford it." Suddenly he brightened. "There a reward in any of this?"

"If we get an arrest and conviction."

"Oh, well. . . ." The man shrugged; it was too tentative and far off to indulge in dreams.

"How many people were in the car?"

"It was a van. Beige, I think. Couldn't see into the back of it. I just saw the one guy driving. I think he had an ulcer."

"He mentioned it?"

"Nope, just kept gulping milk like he'd die without

it. And he seemed the nervous type, you know? Jumpy like."

"Can you describe him?"

The man squinted hard and looked up at the Mobil sign as if for inspiration. "About thirty. Maybe a little older. Dark blond hair, straight and thick—kinda like yours, but not so short on the sides. Good-looking in a school teacher way. Classy clothes, like he had money, but sort of wrinkled, like he didn't care how he looked."

He stared off into space, then shook his head as if making up his mind about something. "Naw, he couldn't of done it. He was a nice guy, you know? Nuts I can spot. I got a sense about people, good or bad. This guy was okay. I bet if you find him, he didn't do it." He shook his head again, this time with more conviction. "Naw, no way. He isn't the one you're lookin' for."

SEVENTEEN

The drops on the windshield expired in the still dust, jigsawing the glass with disintegrating tracks, but the wind brought a steadier spray, and soon the moonlit landscape was obliterated with sheets of runoff from the roof of the parked van. With only the scanty protection of a baggy jumpsuit she was growing cold, but she enjoyed the way low temperatures seemed to strip the world to essentials, and she slid her palms back and forth with the furious rhythm of churning train wheels, building little spots of heat that faded with a languorous glow. Envisioning Phillip huddled within his parka out on the road a few miles back, she wondered whether he would appreciate the benefits of the rain or whether he would see it as foreboding of failure, and she blamed herself for not having insisted upon his remaining in the van. He had seemed well enough when they set off tonight, but his good spells were open to relapse and not to be tested.

How quiet it was without the telltale swish of automobile tires on the pavement. The last car had passed about twenty minutes before, but soon with the rising sun the morning traffic would begin, and she would have to be gone. . . . Scooting over into the passenger seat, she gazed at the highway through a side window, her arms folded along the ledge, her chin on a fist as she recalled how wet and cold Mary Rose had been a few years ago during a downpour in San Francisco when she had lacked the money for an umbrella or a pair of boots. But why did she remember that particular day now?

Because, she thought, if Mary Rose were successful tonight, she would take over center stage. If not, then someone new would have to be pulled from the wings. But in any case she was through with Lisa Ferro. The good doctor had blown her cover and could finally be allowed to drift into the obscurity she deserved. There was no point keeping the bitch alive with a flattering interpretation. Better that the role be disowned and the woman recognized for what she'd really been, not a paragon of compassion and understanding, but a betrayer of the worst sort, one that preyed on vulnerability.

"If ever you're in San Francisco and need help, give me a call," Dr. Ferro had said.

For three months after her prison escape Mary Rose had spoken to no one and lived each day in terror of capture. The only thing that had kept her going was the assurance that if things got rough, she knew a professional who would help. In prison the doctor had probed relentlessly until finally Mary Rose had broken down and confessed a fear of maintaining her sanity long enough to become eligible for parole, six long years from then. Not only had the doctor kept the confidence and not reported Mary Rose's obsession with escape to the guards, but she had seemed sympathetic to a breakout attempt.

When her freedom was a reality and Mary Rose despaired of making it alone, she hitchhiked north and made the promised call. But within minutes of coming face-to-face with the doctor in the sculpture courtyard she had felt it all going wrong. Ferro smiled a tight, professional greeting and scolded Mary Rose for not coming to her office. With practiced generosity that seemed somehow rote she offered her a ride to a halfway house, along with assurances that after Christmas she would be admitted to a therapy program and found a job.

Mary Rose was confused. "But they'd send me back to prison. . . ."

Dr. Ferro scoffed as if at a naive child. "Since when is getting help a violation of parole?"

Parole. Something jolted loose in Mary Rose. The doctor had forgotten her! The warm, loving woman who had feigned the concern of a mother apparently had dismissed everything the moment she jotted it on her writing pad.

Even after Mary Rose had refreshed her memory and explained all the details of the escape, the bitch had remained a bulwark of icy professionalism, going so far as to insist on turning Mary Rose over to the authorities for her own good!

It was a betrayal, plain and simple. The woman had to be stopped. Mary Rose couldn't risk being returned to jail. It was clear that begging would be futile. Pleading never worked on women who pretended to be sweet and helpful, but dropped you like a smelly dishrag. Twenty years ago she had let her mother get away with the same thing, and it had caused nothing but grief. Only a fool refused to learn from her mistakes. She'd been too young and dumb to keep her mother from doing her dirty work. But if she had, everything might have been different. . . .

The day had gone well. Her father's best friend, an older man they called Gramps, had joined them in croquet. Mary Rose loved Gramps because she had never had a grandfather of her own. Her mother's father was dead, and her father's father had abandoned his wife before the birth of his son.

After a final game of croquet and a hamburger barbecue Mary Rose's father and Gramps settled down in front of the television set, and Mary Rose went to bed. Soon afterward she awoke to an awful fight. Her mother had come home unexpectedly and was furious that Gramps was there. She screamed vague threats and vowed to leave.

Sobbing hysterically, Mary Rose ran downstairs and begged her mother to stay, but her mother was deaf to her pleas. Taking her coat and purse, she walked out the door and never returned.

If the bitch had stayed, everything would have continued as usual. All the horrors that followed were the bitch's fault; her father and she were victims of circumstance.

A week after her mother left, her father threw Mary Rose into the closet for the first time. She couldn't say she blamed him. Her insecurity had turned her into an obnoxiously needy kid. She babbled nonstop about her missing mother, seeking impossible amounts of re-assurance. It was no wonder her father couldn't take it anymore. Many times, herself, she had felt like locking up some little monster for a while. Her father only did what others fantasized; it was human enough. He had a lot on his mind, trying to cope with a child alone. But at the time she didn't understand any of that. She showed off to get his attention, cracking jokes and leaning back in one of their good chairs until she fell over and broke the damn thing.

Her dad hadn't meant to be cruel. It was the liquor that made him pick up one of the broken legs to beat some sense into her. He was a simple man; he didn't understand that one could ruin a kid by being too stern. In his own crude way he was trying to prepare her for the hardness of the world. As an adult she could see that, and she was grateful for it.

The important thing to remember was that deep in his heart he had always loved her. A person couldn't feel passion toward someone without loving them in-tensely. If he had really despised her, he would have ignored her. His love fueled his anger. Sometimes she would forget this, and her fury would start to surface, a mindless vengeance that made her ache inside until guilt forced her to recall all the nice things he had done for her, finally putting everything into its true perspective.

Imagination helped her through those dark, endless nights in the closet, letting her escape the narrow walls. In time she learned to assuage the pain by visu-alizing herself as someone else far away: a member of a happy Laplander family herding reindeers, or an Eskimo family hunting seals, or a Peruvian family tending llamas. Her mind could roam for hours and never be bored. It was soothing to be someone else. Magically she could flee the conflicts and agonies of her life for a carefree adventure.

In a way her father did her a favor by forcing her to find respite in fantasy. Sometimes if she remembered, she would hide a book and a flashlight in the corner of the closet in preparation for the next time he'd lock her up. Those were the easiest times of all. During one weekend stretch she read all of *Swiss Family Robinson* and *The Sea Fairies* before her batteries ran out. It kept her from thinking about how unfair it all was—she hadn't really asked for it that time. It was just a case of her father's awful temper. Like a blubbering baby, she had run to him at the onset of her first period, wailing that she was bleeding to death. Understandably he had been unsettled and had struck out by insisting that her mother's bad blood was leaking out of her. He had forced her to douche and douche until she throbbed inside, and then he had locked her up anyway because he couldn't stand the smell of her.

But in all fairness she had to admit that she wasn't one to throw stones. She had a hell of a temper herself. It ran in the family.

During her last confinement she was locked in the bathroom. She had always believed that subconsciously her father knew this would be her longest time and that he was looking out for her by ensuring her access to drinking water. The windows of the bathroom were barred like all the others in the house because her father worried about burglars, but still she could have raised the window and attracted the attention of neighbors.

A reluctance to embarrass her father had prevented her from doing so. It would have made her feel dirty by association. And earlier in the day he had been so nice to her that it would have seemed like a betrayal. For her seventeenth birthday he had bought her some dresses he couldn't afford. She had gotten a lump in her throat unwrapping the package and calculating the extra hours he would have to work to pay for them. Gramps had come over for dinner and had given her some money to go to a movie.

But the film was awful, and she had come home early. Her caution was aroused by the sound of her father's drunken slurs, so to avoid his temper she had sneaked in the back door and tried to negotiate the stairs without drawing his attention.

As she crept down the hall, her father's voice became strangely childish, taking on a high-pitched lisp. Drawing nearer, she could make out the words, which caused a chill at the base of her spine.

"Dad," he was saying, "give me a hug."

She peered into the living room and saw her father and Gramps in an overstuffed chair by the fireplace.

Both were naked. Her father was sitting on Gramp's lap with his head on Gramp's shoulder, planting kisses and snuggling seductively.

Without thinking, she had let out a wail of horror, then bolted to the bathroom and vomited her birthday cake. She was still there half an hour later when her father barreled in even drunker than before. For the first time he pummeled her with his fists, and for the first time she didn't think she would survive. After she fainted, he locked the door. When she awoke, she lay still and listened to the storm raging in the rest of the house, knowing that the pain in her leg refused to subside because the bone had been broken.

She made a splint with the towel bars and bound them tight with adhesive bandage from the medicine cabinet. The ache of hunger passed in a few days. She faced the fact that her dad couldn't let her out this time because he wouldn't be able to face her. His shame in being abhorrent to his daughter would be too great. He had always been a figure of strength to her; the comedown would be crushing. In a way the thought of death seemed a relief to her, an answer to an insoluble problem. She wouldn't mind dying at all.

The bathroom was a nice place. Sunlight kept it bright. Her leg healed nicely; and without moving it she could reach the tub for sips of water and sponge baths. With a bar of soap she marked off the nights on the ceramic tile wall. After fifteen little waxy streaks she noticed that she hadn't heard a sound all day. It worried her that her father might have abandoned her like her mother.

Two days later it occurred to her that she could take the door off the hinges with the tail of her aluminum comb. She didn't know why she hadn't thought of it before.

When she came out, she found what she had suspected all along. For seventeen days she had been thinking that it was the only solution. One of them had needed to die, and obviously her father cared enough for her to spare her life. Confronting each other would have destroyed their love, so it was all for the best. Her father had seen that and hung himself by a nail above the kitchen door.

Hopping around on one leg, she ate something to regain her strength, then straightened up the chaos in the house. To disguise some of her twenty-pound weight loss she put on triple layers of underwear beneath one of her birthday dresses. Then she rehung the bathroom door, dusted the furniture, and hid the liquor bottles in the trash. Finally she called the police.

The one thing she had always regretted was not having the chance to tell her father that she understood. He hadn't meant to hurt anyone. It was okay with her if he needed to pretend; everyone needed a dad. . . .

The rain had slackened, and she squinted through the drizzle to discern the overhead sign that was supported by two-foot steel columns spanning the road thirty feet back. Normally it was lit by ten-thousand-watt mercury vapors, but tonight the lamps were out. The load center had yielded to her crowbar, and the circuit breakers to a flick of her wrist.

Headlights flashed through the rear window, and she stiffened to await the car's passage over the quarter-inch leader cable that was stretched across the three lanes, then threaded through a pulley on the

nearest sign column and laid out along the road to the
van's rear bumper. But the headlights bounced only
lightly as if surmounting one of the periodic breaks in
the road, and then the car was past and gone.

She sighed with worry about the accuracy of Phillip's inside information on this trucking route. The
suspense was beginning to pale, making her edgy and
combative. The tension of being cooped up in the cab
stirred the rage she always felt when confined. She
warned herself not to risk losing everything to her foul
temper. It was her childhood weakness that had
prompted the abuse, her fear that had incited her father's anger. If she could succeed tonight, she would
never be helpless again. Her power would be so obvious and incontestable that no one would dare to
lock her up again. Already she could see changes in
her face from the partial success at Hoover. Phillip
was right to push for this second shot which seemed
bound to exorcize her weakness.

Still, it scared her sometimes, this race without
brakes. But she couldn't withdraw and didn't want to.
It felt too damn fine to be aiming for an omnipotence
that everyone would be forced to acknowledge.

Through the crack at the top of the window the
soapy odor of eucalyptus rode in on the rain, and the
fog of her breath on the windshield began to dissipate
with the breeze. She shook the Thermos to see
whether there was enough coffee for another cup, and
her ring snagged on the embroidered patch over her
breast, its red block letters reading: *Transport Security*. As she carefully disengaged the prongs, the
walkie-talkie on the dashboard emitted the character-

istic burst of static preceding a transmission, and she leaped over into the driver's seat and gunned the motor.

"Two to numero uno," said Phillip in a barking call.

"Yeah," she grinned elatedly. "Whadda ya want?"

"Be sweet, One. This is it."

"Got cha."

"I'm on my way."

With breathless excitement she drove forward against the pull of the leader cable to the white rock marker at the side of the road, and there she jerked to a stop, leaped from the van, and raced back to the overhead sign while pulling on gloves and a little billed cap.

In a moment of tremulous approval she saw that everything had gone well; the leader cable had snaked through its pulley and dragged up a thicker one-inch black steel cable that hung across the road in a deadly parabola. She secured it by attaching its end hook to a ring braced at a height of three feet. Unfastening the smaller cable from the van, she hid in a row of bushes that divided the two directions of traffic—the three opposing lanes safely distant on the other side of a drainage ditch three hundred feet away.

From around the highway's bend three sets of headlights were emerging in close succession as if the vehicles were chained together, and she estimated the speed of the caravan—a transport trailer sandwiched between two escorting automobiles—as being cautiously below the limit, its three drivers taking it easy on the homestretch. In the light of the lead car, sections of the cable were beginning to give off a wan

gleam, and she fretted furiously that the drivers might
see it in time to stop. But the screeching squeal of
brakes came too late.

At fifty miles an hour, with a roaring din of tor-
tured steel and shattered glass that made her ears ache,
the lead escort car smashed headlong into the cable.
Its grille creased as cleanly as a balloon under a ruler.
The transport cab struck it from behind and crushed
it into a wad of junk, then careened sideways along
the cable like a high-wire walker hurrying for the
platform until it slammed into the sign's steel post and
fishtailed its trailer across the lanes. Braking and
frantically swerving, the rear escort car was caught in
a ricocheting sweep and swatted over onto its top,
crumpled to the level of its hood as it exploded in a
torrent of flames that sprayed meteors of metal and
glass into the darkness.

Without waiting for the raging fire to diminish she
drew her gun and raced around the burning wreck to
the front of the crushed and mangled cab. Jumping
up to a side window, she trained the muzzle on the
interior and was relieved to see that force would not
be necessary after all. Within their sealed coffin the
men lay as stilled and bloodied as freshly slaughtered
beef. Transfixed by the gore of death, she wondered
at her composure and thought that by surrendering
their lives so soon the men had cheated her of a
drama.

Checking her watch, she saw that anywhere from
twenty minutes to two hours remained before a general alert would be broadcast, depending upon when
the drivers had last phoned in a location report.

Swiftly she backed the van up to the trailer and un-loaded a small forklift down a ramp.

The popping sputters of a moped blended with the sizzle from the car's smoking hulk, and she peered into the darkness to see Phillip hunched down over the bike's handlebars, his wet parka open at the throat and billowing out behind like a parachute brake. He skidded to a stop at her feet and pushed the bike di-rectly up the van's ramp, then he climbed out and dragged the rain off his face with sopping gloves, as thoroughly soaked as if he had ridden through a car wash. For a woeful moment he stood and stared at the wreck, looking dismayed by what they had done, as feverish and ill as he had been before his remission.

Frightened by his sober gravity, she jerked the pneumatic sheet-metal cutter out of the van and fired up its air compressor. "Hey, let's move it!"

"What?" He licked drops of water from his blistered lips.

"The trailer!"

He seemed to hear through a time delay, but dazedly he took up the cutters and began the work, avoiding, she noticed, any inspection of the cab. Be-hind the crash she strung a row of flares, and then another a hundred feet farther back. When she re-turned, Phillip had nearly finished cutting an opening in the trailer's side, the blades going through the sheet metal as if it were cardboard.

The severed panel yielded to an inward push. Climbing onto the forklift prongs to inspect the inte-rior, she saw that as they had expected, the rear load-ing door was wired with alarms and reinforced with steel bars, but because the trailer had tilted forward like a camel down on its front knees, the three dozen flasks of plutonium nitrate had crashed up against the fore wall where they were easily accessible.

Suddenly she felt Phillip stiffen beside her. She leaned out the opening to see a man running toward them, highlighted from behind by the headlights of his car, which was parked on the shoulder behind the first row of flares. They had anticipated interruptions, and the man's bald pate and spreading gut predicted that he would be middle-aged and manageable. But Phillip looked as if he were entering a coma.

"Never mind," she said calmly. "I'll go."

He gripped her waist with manic force and pushed her back into the trailer, then he stalked off toward their intruder, the two forms merging in silhouette as Phillip's voice drifted back with unexpectedly cool command in recitation of the prepared story.

Wiping the rain from her eyes, she tried to judge how it was going and hoped that if the guy were a doctor, cop, or hero who insisted on helping, Phillip would have the sense to take care of him. Only eight minutes remained.

Not daring to wait for his help, she ducked back inside and pushed the flasks up to the hole in the side of the trailer, turning them lengthwise to keep them from rolling as she maneuvered the forklift into position and pushed the flasks one by one onto the prongs and drove them to the van. She liked the rhythm of the work, the power of the machine.

Driving with authority, she swung the prongs into the trailer's opening, gunned forward, then gasped with dismay as the forklift smashed into a flask and penetrated the metal.

Cursing her cockiness, she climbed inside and yanked loose the impaled flask. As it came free, it fell on its side. She stooped to push it out of the way, but abruptly leaped back with a yelp of pain and jerked off her glove. The sharp, torn metal had punctured her little finger, and the blood from the wound mingled freely with the dark, liquid plutonium nitrate seeping out.

She gave the flask a revengeful kick, then looked up to see Phillip climbing back inside. He seemed to have gotten control of himself.

"Any trouble with that guy?" she asked.

He shook his head, then noticed her wound as she raised her hand to her mouth. Quickly he grabbed her wrist, then scooped up the discarded glove to tie it by two of its finger pockets into a tourniquet below the puncture.

"Hey, loosen it a little," she said. "I'll get gangrene."

Distress widened his eyes, a look of doom so inappropriate to the injury that she had to smile.

"Don't worry, Phillip. I'll disinfect it with a Wash & Dry."

"Plutonium doesn't wipe away."

"Well, what do you recommend? Dry cleaning?"

Silently he glanced at the floor of the trailer where the liquid was seeping from the flask in a dark trail.

She sighed at his reticence. "What're you trying to tell me, Phillip?"

"That you've got about thirty seconds to decide if you're going to give up that finger."

"Are you demented? It's only a tiny cut!"

"You'll live without a finger, Mary Rose. You're lucky it's your left hand. A few years ago in Long Beach a dock worker got some plutonium in a cut and died from cancer because they amputated his arm too late. . . ."

She bolted toward the opening, but he blocked her path. "Come on," he said. "Would you rather die with all ten intact?"

With a disgusted laugh of dismissal she evaded him and jumped down to the road. "Get your kicks some other way, Phillip. There's no way I'm letting you take a knife to me out here."

Grimacing, he reached into his parka up under his arm. "I don't have a knife. . . ."

And with incredulous horror she watched him withdraw his Colt .38 pistol.

EIGHTEEN

John groped for the telephone and jammed down its receiver while his mind reeled from the news he had just received. It seemed unfair, somehow, that things could alter so abruptly while he slept; he felt as if he had been pummeled while still in his corner for the rubdown. He promised himself five more minutes of sleep and dropped back on the pillows, sinking immediately into drugged suspension, the threads of an interrupted dream reasserting themselves and gentling him down until he reminded himself that the telephone call had been real, that he would have to act, and that the safety of sleep was an illusion.

Bolting upright, he stood at stupefied attention while his vision blurred from the sudden drain of blood. Somewhere in California this morning forty liters of plutonium nitrate were in the hands of fanatics.

Colleen rolled onto her back and held a hand over her eyes against the first rays of the morning sun.

"Who was it?" she asked in deep, dead tones.

"No one." He fell back to the edge of the mattress, as if awaiting an attendant to carry him into the bathroom and to prop him up in front of the toilet. But a

sudden bouncing of the bed made him slightly sea-
sick, and he looked over and saw that she was sitting
up against the wall with stalwart attention.

"Anything wrong?" she asked.

His mouth felt full of library paste, and he doubted
that he could open it wide enough to insert a toothbrush, much less to talk. He shook his head.

"Is it about that nuclear thing?" Her voice was
climbing in pitch and clarity, coming awake, and he
wondered how she could dredge up a scintilla of interest when he could barely find the energy to think
about where he had left his shoes.

Pushing off the bed, he stumbled into the bathroom with his feet spread wide for balance, moving as
stiff-legged as a plastic Mickey Mouse toy walking
down a ramp. With pale vigor he tried to shake himself awake, knowing that he would have to be ready
for the next call and hoping that it would be more
informative than the last, which had been sketchy and
melodramatic, phoned in by a distraught agent on the
scene.

With the door left open for the sound of the telephone he stepped into the shower and suffered the
torture of a cold spray, letting the water splash
through the open crack to collect in a puddle on the
bath mat and make an ominous squish when he
stepped out. Toweling off, he pleaded that Mary Rose
not number among the thieves. Let it be anyone else,
he thought, the Prairie Fire League, the Mafia, the
Girl Scouts—just as long as he was not involved. He
could cope when his mistakes resulted in nothing

more then some bookie in Hollywood making a few extra bucks—but not when Hoover Dam might disappear like a popped soap bubble.

With relief he saw that Colleen had gone back to sleep. Pulling on a robe, he skirted the piles of things that were stacked for the move to his new apartment and picked a path to the kitchen.

He had been feeling so good when he went to bed, proud of having gotten the sketch of the man who had driven Mary Rose to Hoover. Admittedly it was a rotten sketch—the gasoline attendant's memory had been vague and fickle, causing continual reversals on details—but at least it had been a start.

And now this. While the Nuclear Regulatory Commission was still conferring on emergency regulations for the shipping of fissionable materials, planning to make a fortress of the barn with the loss of their first horse, there had been yet another escape.

Locating the only remaining pan, he cracked some eggs beside strips of bacon, then rummaged in a packing box for a clean spatula and settled at last on a plastic serving fork. Just in time to seize the kettle from the burner before the whistle could awaken Colleen, he poured boiling water over a smudge of brown crystals in the bottom of a cup, then gasped as she startled him from behind.

"I'll have mine over-easy." She seemed pleased at having spooked him.

"Christ, Colleen—I thought you were asleep."

"Well, if you really expect me to stay in bed, you can't cook bacon." She looped her arms around his waist and leaned languidly against his back with her head on his shoulder. "You gonna tell me what's bothering you?"

"I can't. It's that oath of secrecy you respect so much."

"So what if I swear not to tell, either?"

He shook his head and flipped the eggs.

"You need some butter in there," she said.

He held out the serving fork. "Fine. You wanna do it?"

"God, touchy. Just trying to give you some pointers."

The ring of the telephone spared him a reply, and he ran to take the call in the privacy of the bedroom. The news was mixed. The drivers of both the escort cars and the transport trailer were dead, dispatched by a cable across the road in an old military tactic employed to ambush trucks. But at least there had been a witness at the scene, and the man was fairly certain that a guy who had represented himself as a security escort for the trailer was the suspect in John's sketch from Hoover.

"Anything else that points to Mary Rose Stoval?" John asked dispiritedly.

"Yeah, we got positive identification on the print."

"She left a *print*?" Mary Rose was getting careless.

"No, but it's her, all right. She left a finger."

NINETEEN

The bandage was fresh gauze, but its whiteness seemed to emphasize the wound beneath the cloth. Mary Rose cradled the hand in her lap like a defiled child whom she was trying to lure into an attitude of trust, and whenever Phillip moved too abruptly, she raised her knees to deepen the maternal well. Stoically, she pretended to accept the injury as one of the risks of the game, but her eyes were less forbearing and seemed to unload blame somewhere in his range.

"Still hurt much?" he asked, hating the lameness, but not finding any alternative for his concern. The mood in the laboratory, located in the guest cottage behind his house, was grimly restrained; both of them kept trying to deny their pain, but neither of them succeeded.

"I told you I'm fine." She shot him a look that was defiantly blank, its masked pity aimed not at herself, but at him. He saw her gaze drop to his own hands.

"They're radiation burns, they're not contagious," he said irritably. And feeling defeated, he returned to his work, leaning over the counter to knead the plastique explosive into its two-piece beehive mold, forming a hollowed-out shaped charge.

With morbid satisfaction he watched little pieces of skin from the flaking patches on the back on his hand slough off and mingle with the explosive, becoming an integral part of his creation.

Along with a pair of detonator caps he placed the completed shaped charge beside three dozen others, then slipped into the collapsible sleeves of the glove box and began to filter a crystal precipitate. The work lulled him, coaxed him into a hypnotic float, and eased his pain. He thought how stupid he had been not to build a plutonium bomb the first time around. Timidly he had allowed his concern for safety to overshadow his regard for quality. And in atonement he promised himself that on this bomb there would be no compromises. Despite the greater risks of construction, it would be his masterpiece, the frosting on the cake.

He was confident of a yield in excess of three kilotons. Upon detonation the implosive force of the shaped charges would compress the plutonium core to a critical density, crowding its atoms sufficiently close for the maintenance of a chain reaction, building pressures of a hundred million atmospheres and temperatures of a hundred million degrees while the core began expanding at two hundred million centimeters a second—a pleasing symmetry, that persistence of measurements on the order of ten-to-the-eighth.

Mary Rose scooted over on her stool and studied him complacently, as if finally seeing through some ruse.

"What's your temperature?" she asked accusingly.

"One hundred." A lie; at noon it had been one

hundred and three. Tension torqued his jaw as he fumbled with a sleeve button and pushed up a cuff to scratch away an itch from the rubber gloves, resenting the exposure of his weeping sores as evidence that his immunological system was shot to hell. His hair had fallen out in a bald patch at his crown, and he had taken to wearing a golf hat indoors.

She abandoned her perch and laid a cool hand on his forehead. "Martyr," she said with sweet censure. "Can't you finish this later?"

"It's the last batch." He placed the covered crucible in the induction furnace and brought it up to threshold temperature, allowing its exothermic climb before cooling it and washing away the flakes and salt with an acid bath. As the Geiger counter clicked insistently away, he flipped into his hand the resultant lump of metal, the final portion for his plutonium core.

Greedily she extended a paw for the prize, a look of quiet awe lighting her face as she experienced her first sensations of radiant energy, the warmth of living matter. He smiled like a proud mother whose fetus was taking form, deciding that if his morning sickness were chronic and his delivery fatal, he could accept it as the price of a well-formed offspring.

"I hope you realize," he said quietly, "that I really am going to die."

"So are we all, Phillip. Had you been counting on immortality?"

"I feel it happening."

"What you *feel* is indigestion from the Crisco in my brownies." Her smile was convincingly bright. "Try some Pepto-Bismol."

Casually she tossed back the lump, her eyes crinkling with mirth at the absurdity of the offhandedness, her flurry of nervous giggles pinching at his spine like a pair of ice tongs.

Someone had better stop us, he thought. *And it had better be soon.* . . .

TWENTY

She wedged her toes onto the ledge of an outcropping brick and pulled herself up to peer through the bathroom window. Immediately she saw that her plan was workable, but somehow the reality drained her energy. She was bored by the prospect of creeping to the back door and picking the lock.

Dropping to the ground, she examined the plastique explosive in her canvas shoulder bag with the hope that the sight of her crudely improvised bomb would spur her on. She felt like a kid who had already downed half a dozen candy bars and was trying to get excited about an ice-cream soda. Tying up loose ends suddenly seemed unimportant, and with a shrug of indifference she left the bushes and strolled down the apartment house stairs for the walk to her car.

Over a wig that was gathered down her back in a long braid lay the gossamer hood of a Hari Krishna sarong, the uniform swathing her in anonymity. Inviting only occasional glances of curiosity, she kept her bandaged hand concealed within the flowing folds of the peach gown and adopted the disjointed lumber she had seen affected by some of the cult—an intentional awkwardness meant to indicate an otherworldly focus.

A block from the National Theater she ran into the line for the matinee showing of *The Godfather, Part IV*, and was delighted to discover that the hands-down favorite topic of conversation was the hijacking of the plutonium truck. The line's alarmists speculated on the likely bombing targets, sounding both terrified and tantalized by the possibilities, and attributing responsibility for the theft to everyone from the Rockefellers to men from outer space. Most embarrassing of all was a boy in an SMCC sweat shirt who pretended to be knowledgeable about H-bomb construction for a bored girlfriend who kept nodding absently while stealing glances at a rack of sidewalk tabloids in an attempt to read the lurid headlines.

Sighing with relief that Phillip was not here to witness the triviality of these reactions, Mary Rose crossed the street to the Mercedes, which was parked in front of The Fat Burger. Her sarong drew sneers from a couple dressed in disco gear heading for Dillon's down the block, but she ignored them, anxious now about getting home ahead of Phillip in time to change from her outfit which was so unflattering that she had doned it in secret.

The traffic on Sunset Boulevard was light all the way into Beverly Hills, and she kept to the outside lanes bordering the homes' grassy lawns, which at this time of day were the dappled province of the gardeners hosing away leaves and clippings. As if reviewing the motives of a stranger, she wondered why she had backed away from planting the bomb at the apartment. Was she simply tired of sowing wild oats and entering a more introspective, midlife passage? She recalled having read during her months as a psychologist that there were very few psychopaths over the age of forty, that the disease was one which people tended to outgrow. But she was not yet thirty! Was this precocity on her part? Her lips curled with a smile, aglow with the same pride of maturity she had felt at fourteen when realizing she had finished her final comic book.

But as she turned onto Phillip's twisting, tree-shaded street, she was plunged into sudden gloom. Confusedly she blinked at the vaguely familiar automobile standing in the driveway and at the man knocking on the door with the uptight composure of a professional on a mission.

As if exasperated at finding no one at home, he tossed his head in her direction, and immediately she recognized the traitorous prick. Although stunned to see him there, her first reaction was to be angry at his effrontery in daring to show himself at all.

Staunchly she kept her foot to the accelerator and slid past, hoping to escape detection by any thugs he had happened to bring along. But coming abreast of the property line, she could not resist a backward glance at Mr. John Mezzantia—all suited up in blue like the deceitful fed that he was—and she found herself regretting her moment of timidity at his apartment, wishing like hell that she had proceeded with her plans and wired the son-of-a-bitch's toilet to explode for the kick in the ass he so thoroughly deserved.

* * *

The lines of print gelled into stripes. Phillip squinted to distinguish the letters, but his eyes refused to focus. As if impatient about checking the entries, he turned the logbook to the man behind the counter and named a plane he had used before.

"Foxtrot three seven seven."

The man took in the bandage covering a big purple welt that had emerged on Phillip's cheek during the night, then glanced at the pages in confusion.

"But you can see that it's taken. . . ."

"Well, whatever's available. Any single engine's okay." Feverish and weak, Phillip kept his elbow on the counter for support, trying to shadow his face with the brim of his baseball cap, although the aircraft hangar was bright with midmorning sun. A coating of flesh-tinted makeup camouflaged his skin blotches, and a close crop disguised his scalp's bald patches. But the man cocked his head sideways for a scrutiny under the cap's brim and mumbled something about checking on the plane's hundred-hour maintenance before handing over the key.

Annoyed by the delay, Phillip fretted about his appearance; he couldn't afford an eleventh-hour hitch. He longed to sit, but hesitated drawing attention to his weakness. Delicately he fingered another emerging bruise, surprised that it had blossomed into a walnut-sized lump, visible in the metal trim around the bulletin board as a blood-filled blister.

The counterman returned from the office followed by the owner of Santa Monica Aviation, a rail-thin black woman in her late thirties who had inherited the business when her father and his student pilot tried to make an emergency landing on the Coliseum playing field.

Her hair was tucked into a scarf tied at the back of her neck, and her matching plaid shirt bulged at the breast pocket with pens and a vernier caliper. Possessed by an excess of nervous energy, she moved with quick, deft strides.

"How are you doing, Phillip? Haven't seen you in ages."

"I thought I'd wing down to Palm Springs for some sun."

"Sounds good." Taking him by the arm, she guided him away from the other customers over to a Cessna that was down for repairs. With the authority of one in charge she studied his bandages openly.

"Looks like you walked into a propeller."

He smiled. "I checked my radiator water before it cooled."

As if to pat him in sympathy, she touched his cheek, then flipped off his cap. The movement was so efficient and done with such a presumption of right that it seemed superfluous to be angry. And yet he was enraged. He clenched his fists to keep from socking her in the mouth.

"It's nothing serious." He took back the cap. "Just a reaction to some cold medications."

Her eyes were compassionate, but impervious to rationalizations. "Can't let you fly, you know."

"No, it's really nothing. I've been off the drugs for days."

Knowingly she eyed his hand's patchy skin and his

elbow braced on the counter—which prompted him to snap upright. Faintly he felt himself sway, and he touched a hand to the wall.

"Phillip, you should be home in bed. It'd be criminal to let you go up. You don't have the strength to hold the stick."

With muted fury he argued until she quit responding, and then he tried the grandstand play of demanding that she sell him a plane outright.

"Phillip, go home."

He rankled at the implication that he would destroy her precious planes. "I'll go to World Aviation and buy a Lear!"

When she looked him pityingly in the eye, he stormed to his van in the parking lot and started for home, realizing within minutes that he did indeed lack the energy to fly to Palm Springs, much less to Hoover.

The gas gauge edged toward empty, but he resisted the need to stop, calculating that he could make it on the tank's reserve. Rolling up the window, he turned the heater on low, fraught by waves of chills and nausea that threatened to bring up his lunch of applesauce, the only thing he had been able to keep down. He warned himself to stop dwelling on the humiliation, which only aggravated his illness. If he could just make it home, Mary Rose could drive the van to Hoover while he slept in the back.

In his rearview mirror he scowled at the hoggish woman who had been tailgating his bumper for the last mile up Santa Monica Boulevard. With sweet malice he began to toy with her, slowing until she made a move to pass, then accelerating while the other lanes closed up, then poking along again. Gleefully he savored the image of backing into her little Honda Civic at forty miles an hour, but he resigned himself to playing grab-ass with the little cretin.

During a spree to make it through a yellow light, leaving the Honda to stew on the red, he noticed a woman in a Hari Krishna sarong waving for a ride. A moment later he heard a bump on the right-hand door and turned to see her blurring past. Had he *hit* her?

Awash with dread, he blasted the horn at the car ahead, impelling it through the light while he clung to its tail, watching in the mirror as the woman ran after him, her robes flying, yelling—*his name?* Did she actually know him?

With wide-eyed shock he recognized her all at once. Enduring the honks from the cars behind, he stopped until she climbed in, breathing as if on the verge of a heart attack. Nostrils dilated, she tugged a loop earring from the side of her nose and straightened her wig.

"Who're you supposed to be now, Mary Rose?" he inquired with forced calm. "And where is the Mercedes?"

"I ditched it!" she gasped. "It's hot!"

"Hot? As in *the air conditioning doesn't work?*"

"No, as in *there are feds at the house who'll be putting out an APB on it!*"

He sighed under the sudden weight of the inevitable, a ponderous load from which there was no escape and which in its finality was almost comforting.

"Well, you sure as hell take it in stride!" she said.

"I always knew eventually they'd find us. . . ."

"Oh, God—spare me." She glanced into the back of the van at the bomb which lay secreted under a blanket, its globular mass rocking against foam rubber bumpers. "Why didn't you load it on the plane?"

Wordlessly he pulled into a gas station and parked at the premium pump, his limbs so numb that for a moment he felt himself dissolving. He dropped his head to the back of the seat and let his gaze drift to the clock beneath the station's peaked roof, calculating that if they were to leave for the dam immediately, they would arrive at Hoover before midnight with ample time to act under the cover of darkness, so that by dawn everything would at last be over.

Mary Rose propped an elbow on the seat to brace her head. "Looks like you had a bad day, too."

"The worst." He noticed a female attendant in a white jump suit staring at him through the glass as if uncertain he was human.

"Fill it," he barked.

Visibly starting, she retreated to unscrew the gas cap, then vanished inside on the pretext of answering the telephone.

"Nasty little cunt," he muttered.

"Why take out your frustrations on her?" asked Mary Rose. "Let's keep some perspective."

"Perspective isn't what I lack." In a fit of irritability he banged open the door, marched to the gas pump, and jammed in the nozzle himself. Squeezing the handle for full speed, he sent the figures whirling in frenetic calculation, causing a monstrous back-splash which doused his pants and shoes through to the skin and made his ulcerated patches sting in agony.

Mary Rose and the flustered attendant watched as he sloshed back to the driver's seat, silently assessing his pain.

As an absolute conviction he thought that if either of them uttered a syllable of reproach, he would crawl to the rear of the van and detonate the bomb right here in the heart of Beverly Hills.

TWENTY-ONE

Getting no response to the bell, John rapped on the door, not seriously expecting Dr. Lewis to answer. Lewis's call to the bureau twenty minutes before had carried the background noises of a phone booth on a busy street, and Lewis had sounded rushed for time. Apparently calling on impulse, Lewis had dropped cryptic hints about inside information on the plutonium theft, the confession stemming from a mood John had not been able to pin down, an emotional erraticism tinged with self-conscious restraint, as if the man had wanted volumes to be inferred from his allusions.

After the call John had pursued a hunch and checked to see whether any of Lewis's colleagues in the nuclear establishment had access to the shipping schedules of the Rodale Radiation Lab and had learned that several of them were familiar with the trucking route that had been intercepted the night of the plutonium theft, though none would admit to having broken security.

As his eyes swept the home's well-kept grounds, he wondered whether the elusive Dr. Lewis was one of those financial tightasses who cut every other expense to buy an impressive house. Then he smiled as the Hari Krishna veil of a girl at the wheel of a passing automobile caught his eye, amused by the notion of a Beverly Hills millionaire's daughter taking a stand against materialism in her Mercedes 450SL.

Quickly he gave the bell a few more jabs before cutting around to the rear of the house and peering in the sliding-glass doors of the sunken living room. Jarringly stark in décor, it was carpeted with gray wool and furnished with multiple white couches, polished aluminum tables, and a stainless-steel sculpture that looked like a wilted cactus. Formidable security bars lay in the tracks of the doors, and after rapping on the glass for reassurance of his solitude he set about finding another way inside.

A brick outcropping abutted one end of the house, enclosing a small, interior garden off a bathroom shower. The door was flanked by louver windows, a burglar's delight, and within seconds of dropping down inside he had slipped out enough slats to create a crawl space.

Inside the house was cooperatively silent. He made certain that no one was cowering upstairs, then padded back to the ground floor. Indulging a moment's curiosity about the tastes of the rich, he inspected a game room equipped with a television projection screen that took up half a wall, and impulsively he tried one of the sculptured couches which looked as stiff as a park bench. But the foam rubber beneath the taut velour enclosed him like a mitt around a ball. Somewhat abashed, he bounced up and down a few times before starting off down a long hall.

It led to a kitchen that was incongruously cozy, with cabinets of natural hardwoods, rows of bright copper pots, and hanging plants around a heavy oak table. A search of the drawers in an antique desk yielded a yellowing newspaper clipping that piqued his interest. It reported the death of Mrs. Jerome Oscar Lewis, widow of the millionaire engineering magnate, survived by her only son, Dr. Phillip Lewis of RAM Corp, heir to the six-million-dollar estate.

At the mention of the money John felt a primitive, aching envy, finding it almost impossible to believe that someone his own age could be set up for life. What would it be like to be able to satisfy any impulse?

A note affixed to the refrigerator door with a ladybug magnet caught his attention. A reminder to have Jurgenson's market deliver Oreos, applesauce, and Pepsi—written in brown ink with a flamboyant handwriting he recognized with dread. . . . He had seen it once before in the letter to Jack Smith taped to the door of the *Los Angeles Times*.

The implication overwhelmed him, but suddenly, almost magically, the pieces began to fit together. As an echo from the past he recalled Lewis's voice over the telephone the night of the Hoover blast, a voice sounding groggy with sleep. Now he wondered if the wooziness could have been the first symptom of radiation sickness.

"We're all in this together," Lewis had warned.

TWENTY-TWO

The van was squeezed into a no-parking zone in front of Van Cleef and Arpels in Beverly Hills. Through the windshield's veil of sunlight she looked up the street for Phillip, then checked the rearview mirror, afraid that a cop might appear at any moment. What the hell was keeping Phillip? Waiting here was an insane risk; she should have insisted that they continue on and should not have been meek in the face of his irritability.

Too jittery to sit still any longer, she climbed from the van and stalked past the lavish window displays of Rodeo Boulevard, priming herself to deal with Phillip's foul mood and thinking how ridiculous it was for him to be upset with her for refusing to go to Hoover. It was obvious that they didn't stand a chance of getting anywhere near the dam with the FBI looking for them and knowing their target.

Crossing the street, she peered into Gucci's window, trying to spot Phillip. A salesclerk noticed her sarong and glowered at her over his jewelry cases, as if thinking she planned to chant there the whole afternoon. Spitefully she considered dancing around a little on the sidewalk, but on second thought sauntered off to another window for a better view.

Standing beside a stand of loafers and holding his own gasoline-soaked shoes, Phillip was arguing with a salesclerk, looking as if he wanted to choke the man. Impassively the clerk shook his head. Phillip wheeled around and stormed out of the store with such wrath that Mary Rose cowered in an alcove of the Wally Findlay Galleries until she felt so embarrassed that she ran to catch up with him at the driver's window of the van.

He was firing up the ignition, refusing to notice her.

"Phillip? What's going on?"

Silently he worked his jaw in a struggle for self-composure. His eyes seemed to dry under the force of a hot wind.

"Didn't you get your shoes?"

"No."

"What happened?"

"Nothing."

"Why're you so mad?"

"I'm not."

"You are!"

"Will you get in? Nothing appealed to me, okay?"

She noticed the pulsing of the blood blister against the flakey patches on his cheek and wanted to cry as it dawned on her that he had been shunned in the store for his sickly appearance. Feeling a surge of protectiveness, she wanted revenge. The risk of capture seemed small.

"I'll be right back." She gave his shoulder a determined little pat. "Start thinking of another target, okay?"

His lips pulled tight against his teeth. "Get in, Mary Rose. We're going to Hoover. You'll have to drive."

"There'll be roadblocks!"

"I don't care."

His defiance made her wonder if it was the fever making him irrational. A kamikaze attack on the dam had never been to her liking, but at least it had been a feasible plan. Now they had no alternative but to pick something else. Once the bomb was planted, they could get a hotel room where she could nurse Phillip in comfort while viewing the aftermath of the explosion on television. Hollywood Bowl appealed to her for some reason, but she supposed that Phillip would veto it. He was fixated on targets that were personally symbolic—and his illness made her reluctant to oppose him.

"What about hitting Disneyland instead?" She hoped to make him smile, but his eyes were glacial, as if he were utterly unconcerned about shutting her out. She nodded at the tops of his ulcerated feet, which were red and puffy from the irritation of the gasoline. "Wouldn't you feel better if I got you those shoes?"

"You think I couldn't get them if I wanted them?" He spoke through his teeth.

"I only said—"

"I'm getting very tired of your nagging."

"*Nagging?*" She hated the whine she felt coming into her voice, but persisted anyway, feeling pleasantly perverse. "Is it nagging to help fight your battles?"

His knuckles tightened on the wheel; his face flushed like a mask. Realizing that she had gone too far, she stepped back.

"So I'll just be a minute. All right, Phillip?"

"You're backing out of Hoover altogether?"

"We can't go! It's impossible to get through! They're looking for us!"

"Fine, just so we got it straight." Jamming the van into gear, he roared up the street, then slowed in front of Gucci as if to turn into the parking structure next door. But he didn't make it that far. Cutting short, he rammed straight up over the curb, onto the sidewalk, and into Gucci's double doors, which parted before the front bumper to admit the van, then swung closed behind the tail without suffering as much as a crack in the glass.

Aghast, she looked at the only other pedestrians on the street, a couple of men with their backs to the store who continued their conversation without pause and a young woman in platform sandals with a Yorkshire terrier in her purse who had halted half-a-block from Gucci to stare at the doors, then finding no further outrage to stir her interest, had turned and minced into St. Laurent.

Alone in her astonishment, Mary Rose darted across the street, sailed through Gucci's doors, and followed the tire tracks on the carpet which ran straight ahead to where the van was parked in the women's handbag department. It was attended by a few people rapping on the driver's window, requesting that Phillip roll it down and speak to them. But other than a crushed papier-mâché deer sculpture and a few upturned chairs at the edge of the vehicle's path, the place looked perfectly ordinary. Its chrome-and-glass elegance was intact within the hushed quiet of a bank vault, disturbed by flurries of alarm from some of the clerks. Most of the customers were so inclined to grace under pressure that they surveyed the van as judiciously as they studied the merchandise—as if appraising its value.

The vehicle's rocking suggested that Phillip had retreated to the rear, but he remained hidden by the curtains over the windows. In Mary Rose's attempt to circle the group for a glimpse through the windshield her gown caught the reproving eye of a clerk who refused to let the accident sidetrack him from maintaining standards.

"We don't need spectators," he said with a wave of his hand, as if to shoo out a crazed pigeon that had blown in on the wind.

"Uh—just a moment." On tiptoe she peered through the glass and saw Phillip bending over something in the back.

The bomb? Her mind reeled with apprehension over what he might do. She was shocked that her plans had been so suddenly annihilated, so quickly turned rotten. She felt as if she had been kicked in the stomach and knew she ought to be angry, but she was too confused to do anything but gape.

Backing off from the van, she instructed herself to think, to find some way it could all be undone, knowing all along that it was unchangeable. In a daze she spotted the blue-suited clerk who had infuriated Phillip trapped in conversation with a woman customer, a rail-thin, fortyish blonde.

Lowering her gray-shadowed lids, the woman nodded at his comments, then confided with zeal, "The man looks as if he just escaped Molokai! If you'd let him try on the loafers, you couldn't even sell them back to the alligators!"

The clerk looked mildly offended, but smiled obligingly. "Still, I feel sorry for him. He seemed awfully ill. Someone ought to call—"

Interrupted by the snapping of the van's rear door handle, he fell silent.

Oblivious to the hushed crowd, Phillip stepped out and brandished the detonator as if it were a loaded pistol. In a throaty growl he spoke to the blue-suited clerk, whose face drained to the chalkiness of his linen shirt. Gravely he followed Phillip down a passageway to another department and once there apparently invented a pretext to clear the room, because customers began to filter back like film buffs leaving a disappointing premiere.

Within minutes the clerk reappeared, followed by Phillip, who wore a new pair of tan loafers.

With exaggerated haughtiness Phillip sat on a counter and leaned back on his arms as if to appear cavalier, but his weakness was obvious; he seemed ready to faint

"Now I think I'd like to see some slacks—maybe a wool-silk blend."

The clerk kept staring at the van, as if to puzzle out how this had happened to him.

"Move!"

The shout was shocking in the silence. Mary Rose wanted to melt into the walls, but when Phillip's arms began to tremble, she went to his side.

Embarrassed by her public assistance, he brushed away her hands and sat upright on the pretense of adjusting a shoe.

"I'd like to go," she said.

"Do you mean this isn't what you had in mind about fighting my own battles?" His voice was dry, but seemed to catch in his throat. "I don't need you, you know. You can leave anytime. Maybe you can make Disneyland before dark."

Softly sighing, she noticed that his anger had waned, as if he weren't strong enough to support his passion. His pupils were long corridors of pain, and he seemed to be imploring her to understand. But she didn't want to understand. Only to escape.

On the verge of tears she fled down a hall to the women's department, telling herself that even a man who was going to die could be a jerk! The gall of his condemning them both by indulging a childish temper tantrum!

Dizzy with disappointment, she unwrapped her sarong and pulled a chemise off a hanger. No one could see her; she was all alone in the room, and the hallway effectively hid her from the crowd in the main chamber. Over her dress she slipped a snakeskin coat, then exchanged her dirty sneakers for a pair of pumps with little gold gadgets on the vamps. To hide her wig she tied on a silk scarf, wondering why she had never realized before that her best disguise would be an illusion of quiet wealth. Tacky costumes were okay for schlepping around the Village, but the aura of expensive clothing could put her above suspicion.

As she transferred the contents of her canvas bag to a purse with an eight-hundred-dollar price tag, she came across the envelope Phillip had given her this morning accompanied by warnings not to open it until they were on the plane. She thought about reading it now but decided the message might be sentimental and stop her from leaving.

Without a second thought she marched out the room's exterior door and headed down Brighton Way, her eyes glued to the pavement in distress. But as she walked, her resolve began to falter. She stopped for a moment and held onto a parking meter, then finally turned back.

At Rodeo and Little Santa Monica a pair of wailing police cars screeched to a halt and aligned themselves in a diagonal roadblock across the intersection, and Mary Rose realized that one of the clerks must have gotten to a phone. Evacuation orders were broadcast over bullhorns as pedestrians turned to one another in bewilderment. Half-a-dozen rumors of impending disaster began to circulate, and haphazardly people began piling into cars, accepting rides from strangers.

Mary Rose had the good fortune to be the guest of a man in a Rolls-Royce who took one look at her costly ensemble and felt immediate empathy for her plight. But as they sped away, she was torn by pangs of disloyalty over leaving Phillip alone. With a welling of affection and sorrow she looked back to wish him a silent, fervent farewell: *Break a leg, Phillip.*

TWENTY-THREE

When the last of the police helicopters had buzzed from view, the roar of the rotor blades still filled the empty streets. Stationed at the boutique's front window, Phillip twisted on the detonator plunger's lockring, but kept the unit displayed as a bluff while he scrutinized the building across the street, imagining a dozen or more cops to be in hiding, all of them frustrated to think that cutting him down would generate a holocaust.

It had been over an hour since he had shooed away the last of the Gucci gang. Perhaps he had been foolish to let them leave, but he had been feeling self-conscious about the blast and hadn't wanted his embarrassment to curb his pleasure. Now that the television minicams were in position upwind, at a fifteen-mile distance of safety, he wanted to be sitting alone in the catbird seat, flashing his splendors for the masses to watch on the tube.

In a way he regretted that his final shot at the dam had fallen through, but the thrills of a fresh target and a hometown audience were consolations not to be overlooked. Already his next moves were the focus of a million rapt minds trying to second-guess his mood. Rodeo Drive—the best of Beverly Hills! How fitting that his death would consume his childhood turf! His world would literally cease to exist when he did, like that of an Egyptian pharoah whose servants, pets, and possessions were buried along with him.

Despite his growing weakness he couldn't remember having felt more alive. None of his professional accomplishments had brought the satisfaction of being completely in control, no longer the bright sycophant on federal projects that had the inherent interest of milk-logged cornflakes. He hoped his colleagues wouldn't be too jealous of his monopoly of the limelight. At one time or another all of them had secretly considered the titillating possibilities of a solo nuclear venture, realizing that abilities such as theirs demanded more of a challenge than cutting loose with some dirt and rocks beneath a Yucca Flats mud basin.

In a turn from the window he hesitated long enough to frustrate the cops with a clear shot at his back, then wandered over to the office and considered picking up one of the telephones that had been ringing intermittently for the past half hour. When he had answered earlier, he had been assaulted by a woman's impatient tones wanting to know Gucci's hours, and he had gotten rid of her with the news that the store was closed for remodeling.

Lifting a receiver, he drawled, "Gucci, gucci, goo. . . ."

After a pause the silence was broken by a nervous clearing of the throat. "It's John Mezzantia, Dr. Lewis. You wanted to talk to me?"

"That was then."

"Nevertheless, we had an appointment. Will you unlock the front door?"

"Chance it." He hung up. Had he really phoned Mezzantia about a meeting? When he tried to think why he might have wanted to speak to the FBI, he drew a complete blank, but he supposed it might be true; he had been so preoccupied all day that he had been acting a little crazy.

As he roamed the store, he felt like a kid who had snaked a row of dominoes all over the house and was ready to knock over the first in the chain. In the women's department he discovered a tattered Wheaties box on the counter containing an enormous wad of plastique wired to a ring-pull detonator. His stomach wrenched as he realized it had been abandoned by Mary Rose, and he wondered if she had left it as a gesture of alliance. Had she known all along that their parting was inevitable? Had she opened his envelope and understood that his instructions to read it on the plane were a delaying tactic and that in fact he had never planned to take her to Hoover?

He tucked the box into the back of the van and passed the time by going upstairs and selecting a beige silk shirt and cashmere sweater. The exertion made him feel a little nauseated, but he grinned in the mirror as he added an ascot for just the right touch of drama.

Returning downstairs, he uprighted a chair and sat facing the door with his thumb on the plunger, absently wiggling the toes of his new loafers and considering his impending demise.

To be alive one minute and gone the next seemed magical! He liked to imagine himself being vaporized, then wafted over the city like pixie dust, escaping the indignities of embalmment and burial with a little hocus-pocus. He was so tired that death would be a relief. As a fine powder he would settle upon the city like dust, tenaciously clinging for all time. Anything to escape his mother's fate!

According to the terms of her will he had been contacted by a lawyer after her death, and he remembered being shocked by the sight of her dead in bed, where she had rolled into a ball during a fatal noon nap, like a tiny white mouse with her hands curling up like little paws and her nose wrinkling as if to tweek whiskers. Such a silly and demeaning end!

Of course he hoped that the media wouldn't taint his story with seamy history, but he supposed that his infamy would bring to light some revelations about his parents, prompting a review of all the tritely scandalous deprivations of his boyhood. Without a doubt Mary Rose viewed her own upbringing as a compelling tragedy, but he considered his to be hackneyed melodrama. Unfortunately he couldn't prevent it from becoming grist for the idiot psychologists who would have a field day positing his *real* and *true* motives, wringing dry the neglected child syndrome, with theories about petty drives for filial revenge which conveniently ignored the heights he had climbed.

Brusquely he wiped tear tracks from his cheek as a rap on the glass demanded his attention. John Mezzantia was standing at the door, waiting to be admitted.

Congenially Phillip waved him in, and Mezzantia entered calmly, as if dropping by for advice on an arcane question of physics. But as he approached, Phillip saw that his composure was an illusion, a stance that was convincing because the sun threw Mezzantia's face into shadow and obscured the fact that he was steeled against the confrontation and appeared to have thought long and hard about coming at all.

With a wariness that bordered on the comic he regarded Phillip as if he were a mad dog to be tricked into a trap with the bait of a roast beef.

"Well, John, how's tricks?" Phillip asked heartily. "You here to join forces or just to pick up a gratis cashmere? That suit looks like you put it together from a couple flour sacks."

After cautiously circling, Mezzantia sat Indian-fashion on the floor with the sun in his eyes. A gesture of powerlessness that was amusing in its transparency.

"Where's Mary Rose?" he asked.

"In the van." It was Phillip's final gift: the assurance that she would not be pursued after the blast. "She's feeling a little down in the mouth today."

"Did it ever occur to you that maybe she doesn't really want any of this to happen? There's no shame in changing your mind."

"Sure she wants it to happen! Did you ever try to *shop* in this damn town? A crater will be an improvement in land use."

Mezzantia lowered his gaze, then looked up from under his brows and softly asked, "It was you who tipped me off about Lisa Ferro, wasn't it?"

"I don't recall exactly."

"You wanted to keep her out of this somehow. And yourself, too. That's why you came to my apartment—and why you called me this morning. So at least will you let me try to help?"

"By all means! Say when, and I'll let'er rip!" Phillip hefted the detonator to eye level and grinned with malice.

But Mezzantia refused to be baited. "I understand about the pressures of your job. . . ."

"That was bull. The truth is that I'm really evil. It's simple but fascinating, don't you think?" He smoothed a wrinkle in the sweater.

"What I think is that you're human like the rest of us." His tone was heavy with sincerity, but his eyes remained on the floor.

"Yeah, Charlie Manson and I are saints alike." The guy was beginning to bug him with all the baleful expressions and phony mutuality that were meant to soften his defenses for a surrender. The arrogant presumption of talk about what he *really* wanted was making him think that allowing Mezzantia inside had been a decided error.

As if sensing the ebb of rapport, Mezzantia tried the authority of directness. "How about coming with me now, Phillip?"

"How about splitting alone, John—like right now?" The cat-and-mouse was empty of intrigue, a worn-out diversion whose plays now rankled. And with his loss of interest in the game he found his determination dissolving. He knew that he would have to act immediately to keep his guilt-ridden inner self from sacrificing the title.

"Excuse me a moment." He ambled to the van with a remnant of resolve that prompted Mezzantia to leap up like a spooked pony, hesitating in confusion before he finally tore out the door and raced down the block.

Phillip entered the van through the front door and locked it behind, then crawled into the back and lay beside the bomb. His body curled around the curvaceous mass as if around the haunches of a sleeping lover, and the contact reminded him that he had a place after all, a schedule of his own making. He clutched the detonator and Mary Rose's Wheaties box like treasured amulets. For a quiet moment of double-checking he suspended his determination, weighing alternatives—although there was never any real doubt; he had but a single out now.

And without a qualm he took it.

The blast scooped him up and transported him painlessly into the past, allowing no sensation of the explosion's concussive shock. The messages of agony to his brain were stopped by the severance of their pathways—the outposts and control centers parted forevermore.

TWENTY-FOUR

She ran the massage nozzle from head to toe in lazy repetitions until she had exhausted the hot water supply, and then she stepped from the shower and wrapped herself in one of her bath sheets from Saks, embroidered with a K when she had still been undecided about new first names. Ultimately she had settled on *Janet*, but now she wasn't sure she didn't prefer *Kitty* or *Kris*.

Nude, she examined her body in one of the mirrors that ran floor to ceiling along one wall of the bathroom, **feeling repulsed by her forty-pound weight gain** but rather enjoying the sense of invulnerability and emotional padding which the fatness provided, like the big sunglasses and old turtlenecks she used to wear to fend off the world.

With an affectionate pat to her hefty rump she went to the bedroom and threw open a bank of stuffed closets, selecting a pale blue Halston pants suit that complemented the strawberry-blond cap Sassoon's had made of her hair the week before.

Checking her watch, a divine diamond doodad from Tiffany's, she saw that she had plenty of time before meeting the girls for lunch at Chasen's, and she rummaged through the kitchen cupboards, past tins of truffles, caviar, and mandarin orange slices, to find one of the little bags of Cheetos that she kept hidden in the rear. Certainly junk food was hopelessly déclassé, but one had to eat after all.

Contentedly crunching, she removed a vial of Joy from her purse, then noticed that her wallet looked unusually thin, leaving her almost nothing for her afternoon shopping.

On hands and knees she pulled her old Gucci bag from under the velvet settee and extracted the pack of thousand-dollar bearer bonds, still enclosed in the original envelope because she had been unable to throw away the last memento of Phillip.

In her only form of bookkeeping she made a little check mark on the envelope's corner to signify that she was cashing one of the bonds. And to make certain that they weren't going too quickly, she did a fast calculation. Eighty-two in eighteen months; perhaps a little frivolous, but she had had the original expenses of a basic wardrobe, cosmetic surgery, and the best interior decorator in town.

As always when regarding her fortune she regretted that Phillip wasn't around to share it. Why hadn't they forgotten that damned silly bomb business and enjoyed themselves in style? Wealth really *did* buy happiness. She was so enchanted with the role of well-to-do widow that she felt it would play a lifetime. Disdaining false modesty, she congratulated herself on having grown within the bounds of her psychopathy, like an actress who had graduated from cliff-hangers to genteel comedies of manners.

Whimsically she flipped through one of the rubber-banded stacks, gorging herself on the sight of all those zeros, wondering whether Phillip had decided to set off her hunk of plastique—rather than their wondrous plutonium creation—because he had realized that there was little point in leaving her three-quarters of a million dollars while blowing up the only place in southern California in which to spend it. Or whether he had lost his nerve and surrendered out of guilt. . . .

Of course, who was *she* to blame him for double-dealing? All along she had refused to admit that he was informing the feds, so she wasn't in any position to throw stones about self-deception.

The doorbell chimed.

Automatically, she smiled at the handsome man standing in the hall, aware that she had met him before but not remembering where. The golf course? Her tennis lessons? Suddenly she recalled.

He was studying her with similar confusion and with a diffidence that suggested he thought he was mistaken. But his eyes locked on the bag of Cheetos she had laid on the rim of the antique umbrella stand.

"Long time no see." Now why had she said that? He might have gone away. Was she starting to play Phillip's game of cat and mouse?

He looked grave. "May I come in?"

"Have I any choice?" She peered around for his fellow feds.

"I'm not with the bureau anymore. . . ."

"No? But then you always told *me* that, didn't you. Shall I call you Mike or John?"

Entering with a slight limp, he scanned the room. And in spite of her fears she could not help feeling proud at seeing the apartment through his eyes— although really one could never show off to a man who was so abysmally middle-class, because he could only gape in awe at the overall lushness without recognizing one's better pieces or singling out one's particularly exquisite choices for special praise.

"What happened to your foot?"

"The explosion. I was a block away, but I got hit by flying glass and lost three toes."

"Oh, I'm sorry." She declined to point out that it would have been a lot worse for him if she had left the bomb in his apartment as originally planned. "I can't deny that I hated you for a while there, but it's not in my nature to hold a grudge."

Now where had she left that gun she had bought? Really, she was getting much too careless. Was it still beside her bed? And how could she casually maneuver him into the bedroom? Formerly it had not been any problem, but she had been forty pounds lighter then. . . .

"So to what do I owe this visit?"

"I saw you coming out of Rosser and DeMartino. . . ."

"They're your attorneys, too?"

"I'm looking for a job."

"Well, I'm certainly surprised you recognized me, to say the least. Some of the best plastic surgeons in Brazil would be offended."

"Hasn't anyone else recognized you?"

"Too much bearing. It's off-putting. Anyway, Mary Rose Stoval checked out in the explosion. Or don't you read the papers?"

He was fingering her collections of crystal dinner bells and enameled thimbles, disturbing their positions so that she knew she would have to arrange them all over again. When he spotted the envelope of bonds on the settee, he started to leaf through them as nosy as ever. The man had no sense of propriety at all.

"I never really believed those reports," he said. "The blast made a body count impossible. But I knew that if you were really in that van, you'd have come out to gloat at me."

She laughed, truly delighted. He *did* have a definite charm; it seemed a shame to kill him, but she couldn't very well let him leave the apartment alive. Suddenly she remembered about the gun! She had removed it from the bedroom after reading in *New West* that it was the first place burglars looked and had hidden it instead in the pocket of her long sable in the front closet. Did she dare to propose a walk and go for her wrap?

She noticed him staring at her hands. Abruptly she held them out, palms up and then reversed.

"Can you guess which one?" she asked.

Carefully he inspected her fingers before his eyes came to rest on the left hand.

"Well, you *knew* I'd lost one," she said. "But could you tell otherwise?"

"It looks . . . a little stiff."

"Only if you look *very* closely. Actually it's vinyl!

Can you believe it? It fits over the stump with suction. They made a mold of the little finger on my right hand for a perfect match. The ring is to hide the base line."

She began edging toward the closet. "So tell me! Did you get the job?"

"I didn't want it."

"Oh, well—perhaps it's for the best. You don't strike me as a lawyer. Not straight and rigid enough. If you don't mind my saying so, you're more the wastrel type."

A sly smile; he seemed amused by her insight. "Actually I've been thinking about a hiatus in Hawaii or Polynesia."

"Tahiti's lovely. I wintered there last year." She opened the closet door. But as she reached for the sable, he was standing beside her, pointing a gun at her middle with a look of apology.

"Feeling chilly?" he asked.

She sank to the couch and listlessly munched a Cheeto. "Would you please sit down? You're making me nervous." She glared at the gun. "I thought you weren't a fed anymore. Do you have a permit?"

"No. Just habit, I guess." He glanced over at the bonds with veiled interest.

"Look, let's get away together," she proposed. "We could be in Fiji by tomorrow. In a suite at the Club Med. I'd lose weight. . . ."

He refused to answer. Banging footsteps were coming down the hall, and he rose to admit two of the poorest excuses for feds she had ever seen—a frail

Mexican-American and a petite woman who were certain to have been admitted to the bureau under minority and sexual quotas. But their guns were standard enough, and so too their contempt for John as a bureau dropout. He sank to the edge of the settee and let them take over.

Incredulous, she met his eyes. "*You* called them?"

"Phillip would have wanted it," he said dryly.

Was he for real? she wondered. Such moralistic goody-two-shoeing seemed beyond comprehension. And with fresh amazement she saw that his ethics had strange limits all their own; he was reaching out for the envelope of bonds, revealing for the first time the wedding band on his left hand.

The petite fed moved toward him as if to confiscate the envelope for evidence. "What's that?"

"It's mine." John's voice was as cool as a winter's breeze, but his glance at Mary Rose was warm with irony, and she decided to keep her mouth shut. A snap decision, but it felt right. The guy deserved some compensaton for those three toes—a civil suit settled out of court. If ever she did manage to escape again—and there was no reason not to hope for the best—she would prefer trying to track down the money in Polynesia, to taking a shot at a claim in court.

The frail fed clicked on the handcuffs, and Mary Rose looked her captor squarely in the eye, refusing to show him the expected obeisance or any sign of emotional surrender. Her mind was struggling for spaces of peace like a mother trying to protect her child's innocence in the midst of war. Staunchly she told herself that this time prison would be different. She was a new person, toughened by experience. Incarceration could be a challenge, another situation to be conquered.

If one looked on the bright side, remained flexible about one's role, and kept up a healthy optimism about making the best of things, one could survive. After all, it wasn't the end of the world.

Dell BESTSELLERS

- [ ] **TOP OF THE HILL** by Irwin Shaw $2.95 (18976-4)
- [ ] **THE ESTABLISHMENT** by Howard Fast........$3.25 (12296-1)
- [ ] **SHOGUN** by James Clavell $3.50 (17800-2)
- [ ] **LOVING** by Danielle Steel $2.75 (14684-4)
- [ ] **THE POWERS THAT BE**
  by David Halberstam $3.50 (16997-6)
- [ ] **THE SETTLERS** by William Stuart Long $2.95 (15923-7)
- [ ] **TINSEL** by William Goldman $2.75 (18735-4)
- [ ] **THE ENGLISH HEIRESS** by Roberta Gellis....$2.50 (12141-8)
- [ ] **THE LURE** by Felice Picano $2.75 (15081-7)
- [ ] **SEAFLAME** by Valerie Vayle $2.75 (17693-X)
- [ ] **PARLOR GAMES** by Robert Marasco $2.50 (17059-1)
- [ ] **THE BRAVE AND THE FREE**
  by Leslie Waller $2.50 (10915-9)
- [ ] **ARENA** by Norman Bogner $3.25 (10369-X)
- [ ] **COMES THE BLIND FURY** by John Saul $2.75 (11428-4)
- [ ] **RICH MAN, POOR MAN** by Irwin Shaw $2.95 (17424-4)
- [ ] **TAI-PAN** by James Clavell $3.25 (18462-2)
- [ ] **THE IMMIGRANTS** by Howard Fast $2.95 (14175-3)
- [ ] **BEGGARMAN, THIEF** by Irwin Shaw $2.75 (10701-6)

At your local bookstore or use this handy coupon for ordering:

Dell | **DELL BOOKS**
P.O. BOX 1000, PINEBROOK, N.J. 07058

Please send me the books I have checked above. I am enclosing $ _____
(please add ·75¢ per copy to cover postage and handling). Send check or money
order—no cash or C.O.D.'s. Please allow up to 8 weeks for shipment.

Mr/Mrs/Miss _____

Address _____

City _____ State/Zip _____

Comes the Blind Fury

John Saul

Bestselling author of
Cry for the Strangers
and *Suffer the Children*

More than a century ago, a gentle, blind child walked the paths of Paradise Point. Then other children came, teasing and taunting her until she lost her footing on the cliff and plunged into the drowning sea.

Now, 12-year-old Michelle and her family have come to live in that same house—to escape the city pressures, to have a better life.

But the sins of the past do not die. They reach out to embrace the living. Dreams will become nightmares

Serenity will become terror There will be no escape.

A Dell Book $2.75   (11428-4)